I'm 16, I'm a witch, and I *still* have to go to school?

It's almost Valentine's Day, and everyone seems to be in love. Even Harvey's caught up in the season—but he's crazy for another girl! Now Quentin, the new student from Greece, seems to think I belong with him, but he can't put a love spell on me. I'm too busy trying to figure out how to get things back to normal before I lose Harvey forever!

My name's Sabrina, and I'm sixteen. I always knew I was different, but I thought it was just because I lived with my strange aunts, Zelda and Hilda, while my divorced parents bounced around the world. Dad's in the foreign service. The *very* foreign service. He's a witch—and so am I.

I can't run to Mom—but *not* because she's currently on an archaeological dig in Peru. She's a mortal. If I set eyes on her in the next two years, she'll turn into a ball of wax. So for now, I'm stuck with my aunts. They're hanging around to show me everything I need to know about this witch business. They say all I have to do is concentrate and point. And I thought fitting in was tough!

You probably think I have superpowers. Think again! I can't turn back time, and I'm on my own when it comes to love. Of course, there are some pretty neat things I *can* do—but that's where the trouble *always* begins. . . .

Sabrina, the Teenage Witch™ books

Available from ARCHWAY Paperbacks

Sabrina The Teenage Witch™

All You Need Is a
Love Spell

Randi Reisfeld

AN ARCHWAY PAPERBACK
Published by POCKET BOOKS
New York London Toronto Sydney Tokyo Singapore

This book is a work of fiction. Names, characters, places and incidents are products of the author's imagination or are used fictitiously. Any resemblance to actual events or locales or persons living or dead is entirely coincidental.

AN ARCHWAY PAPERBACK *Original*

An Archway Paperback published by
POCKET BOOKS, a division of Simon & Schuster Inc.
1230 Avenue of the Americas, New York, NY 10020

ISBN: 0-671-01695-4

First Archway Paperback printing February 1998

10 9 8 7 6

Printed in the U.S.A.

IL: 5+

To Beth Reisfeld—
this one's for you; hope you like it

The author "points"—with gratitude—to the coven of cohorts who contributed to this book. In no particular order, they are: Lisa Clancy, Elizabeth Shiflett, Fran Lebowitz, Jason Weinstein, Paul Ruditis, Diana Burke, mcdub, mace, Marvin, Scott, Stefanie, and The Bo.

All You Need Is a
Love Spell

Chapter 1

☆

☆

"I have the most *radical* idea," Sabrina Spellman announced enthusiastically as she breezed into the kitchen where her aunts, Zelda and Hilda, were preparing dinner. "Let's dare to do something totally *normal* tonight."

Zelda, slim, stylish, and matter-of-fact, was standing next to the stove. She aimed her forefinger at a pot of soup, causing the liquid to instantly simmer. Without turning around, she said evenly, "Everything we do is normal, Sabrina."

"That's right," Hilda piped up, agreeing, "Normal for us." Then Sabrina's bubbly aunt pointed at the kitchen table: a large pizza magically appeared.

Sabrina frowned and shook her head. Her aunts weren't getting it. She tried to think of a way to explain it better. Mindlessly she pointed at the steaming pie in the middle of the table, emitting a bolt of her own magic. "I wanted anchovies." Immediately the salty toppings dotted the pie.

Zelda and Hilda chuckled as they joined her at the table. "Being normal is highly overrated," Zelda said as she delicately divvied up the pie.

Okay, so being a teenage witch did have its perks—Sabrina wasn't arguing that one. Instant-gratification dinners notwithstanding, still, there were times when Sabrina just felt the urge to do what ordinary families do. And then talk about it the next day at school like all her friends did. Which she couldn't always do, since no one knew about the pointing thing, or her other powers. So she was thinking, maybe she and her aunts could go out to dinner, order from a cute waiter . . . even send it back if it wasn't cooked right. Or something.

This conjured-up pizza, on the other hand, was cooked just perfectly. Biting into a tasty slice, Sabrina tried her aunts again. "No, I mean it. You guys are always up for a challenge, and I have one. I propose we declare a few hours one night a week—say Sunday, since we could start now—as 'no magic night,' and we'll spend it doing something together, just like the average family next door. . . ."

"Like what?" Zelda arched her perfectly shaped eyebrows and regarded her niece. "The average family next door mows the lawn, burns the barbecued chicken, and fights over the remote control. That's what you want to do?"

"I know!" Hilda was enthusiastically warming to Sabrina's suggestion and waving her hands around.

"How about making it a Blockbuster night? We can rent a bunch of movies, *buy* popcorn instead of conjuring it up . . ." While Sabrina appreciated Hilda's ebullience, that wasn't exactly what she had in mind.

"How about taking the cat for some ice cream?" New county heard from. Salem, the feline formerly known as the warlock Saberhagen, currently serving a hundred-year sentence as a cat for trying to take over the world, jumped on the table and added his two [s]cents.

"Somehow I don't think that's what Sabrina had in mind," Zelda guessed, stroking Salem's back, and his slightly wounded ego. "Right, Sabrina?"

Right. She was thinking more along the lines of going out, just the three of them. Sans the talking cat. Not that she and her aunts didn't ever do things together as a family. Only recently they'd taken a skiing vacation—on Mars. Which was not exactly something she could fully share with her friends. Tonight, she was hoping to do something on a smaller scale a little closer to home. On this planet was a start.

"I know!" Hilda said again. "Let's go shopping! Let's go to the mall!"

Sabrina winced. Even if malls were open on Sunday nights, shopping with her aunts was definitely not an option. Being seen at the mall with parental figures totally crossed the line between normal and laughingstock. If someone from school saw her? Instant mortification.

Hilda's original suggestion was starting to sound better—with a twist. "Actually, Aunt Hilda, I liked the idea you had before: a movie. Only let's go *out* to one. In a theater. Let's look in the papers, see what's playing, go stand in line to buy our tickets, you know . . ."

"I like it!" Hilda responded brightly. "Did they ever make a sequel to *It's a Wonderful Life?* Maybe, *It's Another Wonderful Life? It's a Wonderful Life with a Vengeance?*"

Sabrina sighed and regarded her aunts. They were so different, sometimes it was hard to believe they were sisters. Zelda, a highly regarded physicist, was the practical one: the aunt with the sound advice. She sometimes came off as the disciplinarian, but was always kind-hearted and fair.

Then there was Hilda, the aunt from another realm. (Well, they were all from the Other Realm, actually.) Hilda was a violinist and a pianist. Her passion extended to just about everything, in an over-the-top kind of way. She was the aunt more inclined to give in to Sabrina—or come up with silly, bordering on frivolous, schemes all her own.

Of course, Zelda and Hilda did have a few things in common. Both loved Sabrina unconditionally and had welcomed her into their home here in Westbridge, Massachusetts, on her sixteenth birthday. That was when the witch thing kicked in. They were her closest family members who could guide her in using her newly discovered powers. Unlike Sabrina's own parents—who were unavailable due

4

to geography (her father lived in a book) or biology (her mother was a mortal), Hilda and Zelda were available, full-fledged, mega-experienced witches. Like with hundreds of years of experience. But sometimes it seemed that neither one got out much in a circa 1998 kind of way.

Patiently Sabrina explained, "I was thinking of something a little more current. Something that suggests we live in the *now*. How about the new Tom Cruise action movie? Or that Julia Roberts romantic comedy? Or *Lost In Space?* I'll do the dishes while you guys pick one—just humor me, no magic for a measly three hours. Deal?"

Zelda eyed her warily. "Humor *me* first: Is your homework done?"

Sabrina grinned. "Complete—*plus* an extra-credit science assignment, and *minus* any extraordinary help, if you know what I mean."

That was one of the first things Sabrina had learned—after learning, on her sixteenth birthday, that she was a witch!—there are certain times witchcraft was appropriate, necessary, preferable, or just plain handy. And other times when it was definitely none of the above. Like for homework. Even though that would have been *very* handy at times.

"So," she said, as she pointed the dishes to the sink and disposed of the pizza box in the cardboard recycling bin. "Family movie tonight? Ordinary activity? Without benefit of magic?"

* * *

An hour later Sabrina was almost sorry she'd ever opened her mouth, aside from to eat the pizza. The movie they'd agreed on was the latest Tom Cruise. For some unfathomable reason, it seemed that every "normal" family in Westbridge had chosen that same one. The theater was jam-packed. By the time they started searching for seats—after Hilda brought new meaning to the term "like a kid at a candy counter"—few were available anywhere but the first two rows. Especially not three together. Single empty seats were scattered in more desirable rows all over the theater. In another circumstance Sabrina would have simply cast a spell and gotten people to move over, creating spaces for her party. But even thinking it brought a stern "This was your idea" expression from Zelda.

Shrugging and feigning a smile, Sabrina led her aunts all the way down to the second row of the theater. Even that one was filling up rapidly. As the trio settled into their center seats, the lights dimmed, and the trailers for upcoming movies began.

Sabrina scrunched down in her seat and tilted her head up: It was the only way she could see. Zelda and Hilda did the same. "We're sitting practically under the screen," Zelda complained. "With all sorts of technological advances, I'm shocked they haven't come up with a way to rectify this. It doesn't seem fair, after paying full price. I may see if I can use quantum multiverse dynamics for a solution to this."

Hilda wasn't looking at the situation scientifically. "Better make it quantum multiplex dynamics. We'll be looking right up inside the Robot's nose!" she noted gaily. Then she dived into her humongo-size popcorn.

Sabrina aimed for the up side. "Well, at least no annoying tall people are in front of us blocking the screen." The front row had remained empty. So far.

But just as she said that, a boxy, extra-large man, a woman wearing one of those huge Dr. Seuss hats, and a lean teenage boy in a backward baseball cap plopped down in the seats directly in front of them. They were armed with a truckload of junk: Sabrina silently let Hilda off the hook for all the candy she'd bought. This clan must have emptied the counter. Whatever they couldn't carry on those cardboard trays had been stuffed inside their pockets. The man and woman made a loud commotion as they took off their jackets, ripped open candy bars, slurped sodas, and generally pigged out. The boy joined them in all of the above, except he left his leather bomber jacket on.

Sabrina couldn't believe it! That entire row had remained empty—why'd they have to pick the three seats directly in front of the Spellmans? Even looking up at the screen on a sharp angle, their view would be partially blocked. The man must have been like, seven feet tall with a broad build to match, and the woman's hat alone took up half the bottom of the screen. Unfortunately, Sabrina and her aunts couldn't move over: their row had filled up. They were stuck in the middle.

Zelda was amused. "I don't think it gets any more normal than this, Sabrina."

"Maybe we could ask them to move, and go block somebody else," Hilda suggested as the titles for the main attraction appeared on the screen. She tapped the woman on the shoulder. "Would you mind moving over a few seats?"

The woman whirled around to face them. She was breathtaking. Beneath her enormous funky striped hat, a profusion of silky blond waves cascaded down to her waist. She wore almost no makeup: Her skin was iridescent, as smooth as a baby's, her eyes luminous, her lips, full and lush. Curiously, she stared at Hilda, Zelda, and Sabrina and flashed them an enchanting smile. But her words betrayed the pleasant expression on her face. "No, I don't think so" was all she said to their request. Then she flipped around to face the screen.

Zelda's patience was waning. Annoyed, she leaned forward and tapped the woman on the other shoulder. "Fine, but could you at least take your hat off? You're completely blocking our view."

Again, the woman turned and favored the three-some with a dazzling beam. Again, she simply said, "No, I don't think so." And went back to the movie.

"How rude!" Sabrina was outraged and started to point her finger. Zelda quickly covered it. "Uh-

uh. No magic, remember," she whispered. "Let's see, what would a *normal* person do in this situation?" Sabrina wondered if her aunt was testing her for that ridiculous no-magic idea.

"Call the manager over?" she guessed.

"Normally," Hilda answered, accenting that word, "but do you really think you have a shot at getting anyone's attention—or even getting out of the aisle?" Hilda was right. There was no way they could summon an authority, not from where they were. And getting out would not only be tricky, but time consuming. The row was filled with families, many of whom had littered the floor with coats, totes, candy wrappers, popcorn boxes, and soda cups. Plus, the movie was starting and Sabrina didn't want to miss the beginning.

Frustration was not something she tolerated well. Using witchcraft against obnoxious people was usually sanctioned, if just to teach them a lesson. It was Sabrina who'd put the kibosh on that—for the next two and a half hours, anyway.

Grumpily Sabrina withdrew her half-outstretched digit and folded her arms across her chest. She squirmed this way and that, trying to find a position where she could see the screen. From any angle all she got was a random nostril, or at best, half of Tom's face. Her aunts were similarly searching for the best position to see something. Anything.

This was not exactly how she'd envisioned her

normal evening out with the folks. Gamely she tried to enjoy the movie. What she could see and hear of it.

"Martin, I said *I* wanted the popcorn!" the hat-charged woman hissed loudly as her giant husband blithely stuffed his face.

"Get your own, Veronica!" he finally responded, swatting her hand out of the way. She proceeded to elbow him right back and grab a handful of popcorn.

"Save some for me, Dad," the son insisted, leaning over his mother to rudely grab some from his dad.

Sharing didn't seem to be Martin's strong suit. He was very territorial about his popcorn. "Quentin, you had your chance when we got here. You didn't want any then, you can't have mine now."

"But I wasn't hungry then," Quentin whined. "I'm hungry now. C'mon, Dad, give it up!"

Martin had a temper, and he'd clearly had enough. "You want some? Here!" he thundered, and proceeded to hurl the popcorn full force at his wife and son.

Sabrina's mouth fell open. She'd never seen such infantile behavior—not even at school where lunch-time food fights were pretty much the boredom-buster of choice. Her aunts were similarly astounded, as was everyone in their immediate area. Hilda even started to get up to help the wife brush herself off. But Veronica didn't need Hilda's help. Once engaged, she and her son Quentin gave as good as they got. The two of them started flinging candy Jujubees at Martin, who just laughed at them, shouting, "You want war? I'll give you war!" And leaned over to grab his soda. It was the bonus size. That's when Veronica and Quentin retaliated with their sodas and an arsenal of Milk Duds, Chuckles, Snow Caps, and Starbursts. Everything went flying! On top of which, they were screaming insults at each other. An all-out war had actually begun!

Quickly Sabrina slid down in her seat and covered herself with her jacket. No way was she about to get drenched with sticky soda from these fractious rabble-rousers. She was *so* tempted to teach them all a lesson . . . a tiny little point of the finger was all it would have taken. She knew Hilda was thinking the same thing. But a glance over at Zelda told them both to forget it.

Besides, she was sure someone must have summoned the manager by now—the entire front half of the theater was up in arms at the antics of the boorish bunch. Cries of "Sit down! Shut up! Get out!" resounded throughout the theater. To which the threesome rudely yelled right back, "Mind your own business! Leave us alone!" And proceeded with their battle.

Tom Cruise, up on screen, didn't stand a chance.

Just as Sabrina dared to peep out from under her jacket, her eye caught a full-face view of the boy they'd called Quentin. Sitting behind him, she had noticed blond curls escaping from beneath the brim of his backward baseball cap. Now that she could see his face, she gasped involuntarily. His smooth, round, dreamy face was ringed by blond curls, his eyes twinkled under long, thick eyelashes. He actually flashed her a deeply dimpled, full-lipped smile before he went back to flinging Milk Duds at his enraged dad. Involuntarily Sabrina's heart quickened. He was gorgeous! All he needed was a personality transplant.

Finally, after what seemed like an eternity, the manager—with back-up security—did come flying down the aisle to eject the clamorous clan. Which took a while, since Martin, Veronica, and Quentin felt their behavior was normal and appropriate, instead of disruptive and wildly inappropriate. Eventually, however, they were escorted out of the theater. Not before Quentin shot Sabrina another dazzling smile over his shoulder, though. She had the weirdest feeling: almost as if this whole calamitous charade had been staged for her benefit. But that was ridiculous.

Bowing to audience demand, the manager agreed to start the movie all over again. Hilda looked at her watch. And then at Zelda. Sabrina understood: three hours was up. The self-imposed "no magic" ban could be lifted. The three witches immediately "enabled" themselves to more desirable seats, from which they enjoyed the movie immensely.

Later, as they left the theater, Hilda and Zelda actually complimented Sabrina on her idea. "Let's do this more often," Hilda said. "Only let's eliminate the no magic part."

"Agreed," said Sabrina, adding, "You guys were right. Being normal is highly overrated."

Truthfully, Sabrina was actually psyched at tonight's events. She'd have something cool to tell her friends at school tomorrow to answer the inevitable, "What did you do this weekend?" question. And this time, Sabrina wouldn't have to eliminate the fun parts.

Chapter 2

Telling her friends about Sunday night's theatrical experience was exactly what Sabrina was doing the next morning in Mr. Pool's first-period science class. Make that, trying to do. Mr. Pool must have been detained, so the leaderless class got a few extra minutes to socialize. They were making the most of it. Sabrina twisted all the way around in her seat to talk to Jenny Kelly, her best friend, who sat behind her.

"You will not *believe* what happened last night, when my aunts and I went to the movies..." Sabrina started.

That's when Libby Chessler, Sabrina's least favorite friend, leaned across the aisle to break in, "Guess who asked me to the Valentine's Day dance? I'll give you a hint: Larry Carson! As in, star quarterback of the football team Larry. In fact, *I* went to the movies with *him* last night. *I* wasn't reduced to going with my maiden aunties. . . ."

Libby was always trying to one-up Sabrina, and usually she succeeded. Libby—with the glossy, long, dark locks and straight-out-of the Bisou Bisou boutique clothes—was Westbridge High School's most popular, boy-magnet head cheerleader. Not only did she know it, she flaunted it. Libby had taken an instant dislike to Sabrina from the first day of school. "Freak, loser, and geek," were a few of the less inventive epithets Libby routinely tossed Sabrina's way. Only sometimes did Sabrina allow herself to toss a few *pointed* lessons Libby's way.

Jenny, on the other hand, knew the score. She and Sabrina had completely bonded from day one and had been instant best buds ever since. Jenny was unaffected and totally down to earth, from her unprocessed curls, to her uncomplicated clothes to her unaffected attitude. They could tell each other everything—well, almost, anyway. They let Libby brag for a few minutes, and then tuned her out.

"So go back to what you started to say, Sabrina, about the movies last night?" Jenny urged, sincerely interested.

Sabrina checked her watch: the class should have begun five minutes ago, and still Mr. Pool was AWOL. No substitute or announcement over the PA system, either. Which was strange. Still, it did give her time to tell Jenny all about the family food fight between the bizarro bunch—Martin, Veronica, and Quentin. Sabrina couldn't hide her smile, however, when she described Quentin.

"He was *so cute,* Jenny—and like the rest of his family . . . *so* obnoxious!"

Jenny sighed. "Isn't that always the case? The cute ones know it, and flaunt it. Rendering them obnoxious and, therefore, unappealing."

"Well, not all of them," Sabrina quickly answered, glancing a few seats over toward Harvey. Just as she'd made a friend and a rival that first day of school, so she'd fallen for her first crush: Harvey Kinkle was super cute, and not at all obnoxious. Harvey was sweet, and modest. He didn't have a devious bone in his body, and he liked everyone, easily and openly. Right now he was in an animated conversation with the school nerd, Melvin Bibby.

Harvey was also an athlete—unlike Larry he wasn't exactly a star, but maybe someday he'd be off the bench, if he worked really hard at it. Harvey and Sabrina had fun together, listening to music, playing foosball, and hanging out after school at the Slicery. They'd started out as great friends and seemed to be stuck in Platonic-ville forever. The biggest obstacle to their romance had been Harvey's initial cluelessness. He didn't seem to get that Sabrina really, really liked him—or that he felt the same way about her. It had taken months for him to see the light, and then weeks to act on it. When he finally did, another obstacle was thrown in their path: Sabrina's kiss turned Harvey into a frog!

Well, life as a teenage witch *did* have its complications. But when true love is based on friendship, as Sabrina found out, it can overcome anything, even temporary amphibian-itis. Now, the two of them were semi-officially boyfriend and girlfriend. Not that Harvey had asked yet, but Sabrina assumed she'd be going to the Valentine's Day dance with him. It was several weeks away, however, and long-range planning wasn't Harvey's strong suit.

Suddenly Jenny's voice interrupted Sabrina's reverie. Sabrina refocused on her best bud. Jenny had a weird look on her face. "This boy from the movies last night—you said he had curly blond hair, right?"

"More like golden ringlets," Sabrina acknowledged.

"And twinkly blue eyes?"

"Peering out from under the longest lashes," she answered, remembering when he'd flashed them on her.

"Dimples, leather jacket, backward baseball cap?" Jenny was ticking off all the characteristics Sabrina had just described. "Anything else you remember about him?" Jenny asked.

Why was Jenny so interested? It's not as if she wants to meet this kid, obnoxious as he'd been. And it's not as if they'd ever see him again. . . .

"What's with the microscopic intensity of your interest, Jenny?"

"I was just curious . . . did he look anything at all like . . ." Jenny pointed directly to the front of the classroom and Sabrina whirled around. ". . . him?"

There stood Quentin.

In the flesh. Wearing that same leather jacket over a stonewashed denim shirt and carrying something resembling a violin case. Golden curls framed his angelic face. He was luminous, breathtakingly cute. A fact which did not escape the female members of the class as conversations halted, some midsentence.

He was standing alongside Mr. Pool, who seemed slightly taken aback at the class's sudden, rapt attention. Lanky in a beanpole kind of way, Mr. Pool was Sabrina's favorite teacher. "Sorry I'm late, class," he was saying, "but I was summoned into Principal Conroy's office to personally escort our newest student into the class. I'd like you all to welcome Quentin Pid to our school. Quentin is a transfer student. He comes to us from Greece . . ."

From Greece? His English was perfect at the movies last night. Sabrina was more confused than intrigued. *And he's so blond! Aren't Greeks usually dark?*

"This is his first day at our school," Mr. Pool explained, "and this is his first class. So it's up to you to make his first impression of Westbridge a favorable one. Let's find you a seat, Quentin, and then I'll pair you with a buddy to get you up to speed on our work."

As Mr. Pool started to direct Quentin to an empty seat, the new boy zeroed in on Sabrina. And he did it again: flashed her that dazzling, dimpled smile. It unnerved her.

"Hmmm," Jenny murmured, "looks like he remembers you, too, Sabrina."

"Remembers you? From where?" Libby's cute-boy radar went into effect. She pushed her way into the conversation, demanding impatiently, "You know him? How come you didn't say anything?"

Sabrina shot her an annoyed look. "I didn't say I knew him. *I started* to say I sort of saw him last night. You remember, when I was at the movies with my 'maiden aunties' . . ."

After Mr. Pool had settled Quentin into a seat, he walked briskly up to the front of the classroom and flipped through his notes, musing, "Let's see. Sabrina, you're my best science student—would you be available to tutor our new student?"

Before Sabrina could answer, Libby's arm shot up. She didn't wait to be recognized but blurted out, "I'll tutor Quentin, Mr. Pool, I'm more available than Sabrina. She has to take care of her . . . aged aunts. Besides, I'm getting all A's. And *I* would be sure that Quentin's first impression of our school is accurate. *I* know practically everyone . . . who's anyone . . . I could introduce him around."

Mr. Pool shrugged his narrow shoulders. "I guess if you're that eager, Libby, go right ahead." Libby favored Sabrina with a self-satisfied smirk.

Sabrina wasn't sure what she felt. She was steamed at Libby—but for what? Quentin was obnoxious—she wouldn't even have *wanted* to be his study-buddy. Let Libby feel like she got the upper hand. Libby was in for a big surprise as soon as Quentin showed his true colors.

But as weirdness would have it, Sabrina was the one in for a surprise. As the day wore on, Libby practically Velcroed herself to the cute new transfer student, and did indeed show him around—her way. Before the final bell rang, Quentin, who, of course, spoke perfect English, met Libby's clique, Jill and Cee Cee, the entire cheerleading squad, and several members of the football team. Libby insisted he sit with the popular kids at lunch, and even saw to it that his locker assignment was right next to hers—even though that meant several kids had to switch theirs.

From what Sabrina could tell, Quentin acted like a perfect gentleman throughout. While completely charming and gratefully receptive to all Libby's introductions, he apologized to any students whose lockers were displaced on account of him. There was no sign of the whiny, disrespectful, food-flinging brat from the movies the night before.

There was still no sign of that side of him as the week drew to a close. Instead, Quentin quickly ingratiated himself with the school's populace. He attracted swarms of students like bees to a honeycomb. And Quentin seemed to revel in his instant celebrity—but not in an obnoxious way at all. He was a complete charmer.

So complete that all his teachers were cutting

him an incredible amount of slack on the "learning curve." It was just his first week, but his English was perfect since he'd gone to a pricey, private school in Greece rumored to be ahead of Westbridge's curriculum. Yet, according to what Sabrina was hearing, he was getting away with academic murder: He could skip assignments and hand in half-done homework. Even Mr. Pool excused him from a lab experiment and told him he could take a makeup test on Friday.

The entire female student body at Westbridge seemed enraptured by him. Quentin was a girl-magnet—the instant crush of half the school. Sabrina had heard there was a competition in the works already for who would ask him to the Valentine's Day dance first. Which Libby was ironically out of.

"Libby didn't do herself any favors lining up a date with Larry for the dance," Sabrina noted as she and Jenny strolled across the school quad during nutrition break on Thursday of that week.

"For once, Libby outfoxed herself," Jenny agreed. Casually, Sabrina's best friend added, "which makes Quentin fair game for any of us."

Sabrina stopped in her tracks. "Any of us? *You* can't be thinking of asking him, Jenny? Not after what I told you!"

Of all the girls she knew, Jenny was the least likely to fall for a boy based on looks alone. Pure-hearted, truth-seeking, ethereal-girl Jenny wasn't prone to crushes on cute boys: it was against her

21

principles. "Looks count for nothing. It's what's in his heart, soul, and intellect that counts," Jenny was always saying. Sabrina admired Jenny's idealism, although it did make it hard for her best friend to find dates in high school.

Jenny pursed her lips. "Let's put it this way. I'm reserving judgment. Quentin's been here less than a week—so far he's been a complete doll. If some girl doesn't act quickly, he'll be taken."

Sabrina was about to remind Jenny that Quentin was a class-A brat, when someone came up behind the girls and tapped her on the shoulder. For a split second she thought it might be Quentin.

She actually flinched when she heard Harvey say, "Who'll be taken?" as he fell into step with the girls. Quickly she brightened. Harvey was wearing an oversize sweatshirt and loose-fit jeans. He looked especially adorable.

"Oh, Jenny was talking about Quentin. There's apparently some dumb competition for who's going to ask him to the Valentine's Day dance."

In a sense Sabrina was glad for the innocent segue into the dance. Maybe Harvey would realize it was just a few weeks away and he hadn't officially asked her yet. But instead of going, "Speaking of the dance, Sab"—Harvey often called her that; Sabrina thought it was cute—"I assumed we'd go together," he dug into his backpack, extracted a bag of chips, and said, "No kidding. That doesn't surprise me at all. Girls are like gaga over the guy."

As the threesome settled in on their favorite

bench, Sabrina bristled. "Can you even believe that? I mean, he's been here less than a week. And as I told both of you—no one really knows what he's like yet."

Of course, Sabrina had told Harvey about her movie experience, but like Jenny, he seemed almost to disbelieve her. Harvey accepted Quentin at face value: that he was just a cool guy. In fact, none of the boys at school seemed threatened by this hot newcomer and, amazingly, didn't act like jerks around him.

Only Sabrina, it seemed, remained steadfast in her suspicion of him. And she wanted to prove her point that Quentin was not what he seemed. Turning to her friends, she demanded, "How come he never takes that jacket off—he's worn it every day!" Okay, Sabrina knew that was lame, but so far, it was all she had.

Harvey shrugged and munched on his chips. "Hey, it's a cool-looking jacket. If I had one like that, I might wear it all the time, too."

Jenny, whose snack of choice was trail mix, brushed off Sabrina's observation. "What's wearing a jacket got to do with anything? Maybe he's insecure. Maybe it's like holding on to a teddy bear or something. It is his first week at a new school— in a whole new country. Cut him some slack, Sabrina."

Leave it to Jenny to look for deeper significance, Sabrina thought. But she knew what she'd seen. Not only had Quentin been a brat at the movies, he

23

enjoyed taunting his parents, goading them on. He relished being rude and raucous and creating a ruckus. Hadn't his dazzling smile told her that? No, she was not about to be suckered into joining the Quentin Pid fan club. She tried to think of something else that proved his weirdness.

"Okay, forget the jacket. What's in that strange case he's always carrying around with him? Does he play violin or something?"

Harvey knew the answer. "That's not a strange case, Sab. It's an archery case. It holds his bow and arrows. He joined the archery team."

"Really?" Jenny seemed impressed. "He's an athlete? He does look kind of buff." She nearly swooned.

But Sabrina wasn't buying it. "Wait a minute: I've seen our archery team. And their bows wouldn't fit in that case—it's too small."

Harvey shrugged. "He's using his own equipment. Brought it from Greece. Coach said he insisted. And since he tried out with it, and made the team, there's no rule that he has to use standard issue school supplies. Besides, he was elected captain yesterday."

It made sense, but Sabrina wouldn't give up. "Archery? Isn't that our hurting-est team? I mean, if he's such an athletic superstar, why not the football team? That's where the glory is."

Harvey shook his head. "What's the deal, Sabrina? This isn't like you. Why are you so determined not to like him? Just because of one tiny incident at the movies? And from the way you described it, it almost sounds like his parents were the nut cases. Maybe—if it even *was* him—he was just reacting to them."

"If it even was him?" Sabrina was startled. "You guys think I don't know what I saw?"

Jenny sided with Harvey. "Really, Sabrina, Harvey has a point. Doesn't everyone act differently around parents? I mean, most parents have the innate ability to bring out the worst in us. Maybe what you saw was some temporary insanity thing: an aberration. It can't be easy just moving to a new country. Maybe they were all tense and it just exploded at the movies. Maybe it's even a cultural thing: Greeks think it's okay or something to blast each other at the movies. Again, even if you're absolutely sure it was him."

"Even if I'm absolutely sure that was really him? A cultural thing? Jenny! Harvey! Come *on,* you guys!"

But her two best friends were not convinced. "Innocent until proven guilty, Sabrina," Jenny said. "That's what makes *this* country great." Then Jenny and Harvey actually high-fived each other!

Sabrina was getting frustrated. "It's proof of his brattiness you want? Okay, proof you'll get."

☆

Chapter 3

☆

Sabrina knew she was being a little obsessive, but she was determined to force Quentin to reveal his true colors. It seemed important to her. When she'd told her aunts about the amazing coincidence of the movie brat enrolling in her school, and the apparent turnaround in his behavior, Hilda and Zelda were not as suspicious as Sabrina.

"Maybe he and his family were just having an off night," Zelda theorized. "Mortals can act awfully strange at times, then feel remorseful and reverse themselves. It happens all the time."

"It happens with witches, too," Hilda added. "Look how many times Drell has reversed himself." Drell was the fearsome, all-powerful head of the Witches' Council, but Hilda wasn't referring to the sometimes quirky judicial decrees he routinely handed down: She meant his on-again, off-again romantic history with her. Including the time he left her stranded at the altar.

"Unfortunately, our Machiavellian leader has yet to reverse his most damaging decision—the one that turned me into a cat," Salem sniffed.

Her family had the most annoying way of changing the topic.

Sabrina decided to confront Quentin. But something told her he wouldn't come clean in public; being alone with him was her best shot. Which Libby was making pretty much impossible. Then Sabrina remembered the makeup test Mr. Pool had offered him. After eighth period on Friday, Quentin could be found in the science classroom. She decided to wait until he was done and Mr. Pool had left.

But when Sabrina peeked through the windowed door to the science room Friday afternoon, there was no sign of Mr. Pool at all. The blond transfer student was there, all right—alone. Quentin was sitting at his desk, staring out the window. Still wearing his leather jacket and backward baseball cap, the ever-present archery case propped up by his feet. His number two pencil was poised between his thumb and forefinger—almost as if he was ready to send it flying. The test paper lay in front of him. Assuming he was finished, Sabrina boldly stepped inside the classroom. He didn't see her at first, nor did he appear to hear her approach his desk.

Sabrina spoke up quickly. "Hey, Quentin. I think I may be the only one at school who hasn't officially welcomed you to Westbridge. And, of course, to America."

He spun around to face her, but his face registered no trace of surprise. Involuntarily Sabrina gasped. He was . . . she tried to find the right words. Not handsome in a classically sculpted way. More like . . . beautiful. In an ethereal, dreamy way. His words jolted her back to reality.

"Sabrina," he said in a low, conspiratorial whisper as he leaned back in his seat. "Finally. I wondered how long it would take you to come to me. Although, I have to admit, I did imagine your hair would be a lot longer."

Come to you? Sabrina was bewildered. My hair would be longer? She tried not to let her confusion show, and ran her fingers through her straight blond shoulder-length hair. She went for a breezy quip. "Well, it's been kind of hard getting near you, Quentin. I practically had to take a number."

He didn't respond to her cute response. All of a sudden she felt awkward. "So, uh, Mr. Pool said you're from Greece. What's Pid short for? Pideapolis or something?"

Quentin's periwinkle-blue eyes sparkled as he stared at her. It was unnerving. "It's not short for anything, Sabrina. What's *your* real name?"

This conversation had gone from awkward to weird in a nanosecond. Almost defensively she answered, "Sabrina Spellman. But that's not surprising. It's an All-American name, just like me. An All-American girl."

"Are you really?" Quentin asked curiously, still staring at her. "Somehow I didn't think so. *I* have a confession to make, Sabrina Spellman. You've put a spell on me, I think. . . ."

Sabrina's knees suddenly went weak—*he couldn't know*. She braced herself on the nearest desk.

If Quentin noticed her panic, he didn't show it. ". . . what I meant to say is, I really like you, Sabrina Spellman."

Quickly she pulled herself together. "Uh, that's really, really sweet, Quentin, but look, let's stop kidding each other. I saw you at the movies . . . and you saw me. I know you're not as . . . well, nice and sweet as everyone thinks you are. Are you?"

Suddenly Sabrina wasn't sure what she thought about Quentin. Especially after he chuckled, "Are any of us *really* what everyone thinks we are?"

Again, Sabrina steadied herself on the desk. *What was he saying?* Quentin didn't give her a chance to respond. "Of course, that was a rhetorical question. Anyway, as I was saying, Sab . . . is it okay if I call you Sab? I really like you and would be honored if you'd go to that Valentine's Day dance with me."

This time Sabrina had to sit down. She didn't trust her legs to support her. She was in the Twilight Zone, right? This was the most surrealistic conversation she had ever had—and that was saying a lot. She, after all, had visited other realms. She regarded Quentin. His angelic face appeared innocent, open. He was actually waiting for an answer.

Sabrina pulled herself together. "Actually, Quentin—I'd prefer if you didn't call me Sab. It's kind of a pet name my boyfriend has for me. And besides, you don't even know me. How could you possibly *like* me? I, on the other hand, witnessed your immature behavior at the movies and . . ."

Quentin's jaw fell open. His eyes widened. Sabrina didn't know exactly what he was reacting to, but suddenly Quentin appeared unsteady, like *he* was in major shock.

"You . . . you have . . . a . . . boyfriend? But that's . . . impossible," he stammered.

Sabrina didn't know how to react. Libby probably told him she was too much of a loser to have a boyfriend—but hadn't Quentin just said he liked her? So he couldn't be buying into Libby's nonsense. Why was he so shocked, then? Maybe he just had a king-size crush on her and was bummed to find out she wasn't available? Had he not, after all, shot her a series of dazzling smiles? Starting that night at the movies.

Sincerely she said, "Look, Quentin, I'm sorry to disappoint you."

Suddenly Quentin's tone was a mix of tenuous and ominous as he tapped his fingers on the desk and quietly demanded, "Who's . . . who is it? Who's your boyfriend?"

Sabrina felt unsure about answering him. But here it was: The tiniest bit of the jerk she'd seen at the movies was on the verge of emerging. If she told him, she could draw the rest out and prove to her friends that she was right all along. Sabrina drew in her breath. "His name is Harvey Kinkle," she answered confidently. "And I'm going to the Valentine's Day dance with him."

"He asked you already?" Quentin's cherubic face had started to redden.

"Not yet. But it's early. He'll get around to it."

Quentin did not compose himself. He remained flushed, flabbergasted, flummoxed. Abruptly he grabbed his archery case, jumped up, and stormed out of the room. But not without a parting shot. "You just *can't* have a boyfriend, Sabrina. It isn't possible. Don't be surprised if that Harvey person doesn't get around to asking you to that dance." Quentin sounded almost . . . desperate.

Quentin Pid was not happy. He did not deal well with frustration, either. When he returned to his new home on Mount Olympus Lane, he exploded at the first person he saw: his mother. Veronica Pid was languidly stretched out on an overstuffed sofa, reading *Men Are From Mars; Women Are From Venus. Well, duh,* she thought, in the current vernacular. *These people are just getting around to this news-flash? Just how behind are they, anyway?* She barely noticed her son stomping into the house.

Until, that is, Quentin ripped his cap off and

flung it in her direction with such force it nearly knocked the book out of her hands. He tossed his archery case to the ground and stormed around the room. "This isn't working!"

His mother struck a bemused pose. Gently she put the book down and regarded her hot-tempered son. He had so much of his father in him. She tapped on a throw pillow and softly murmured, "Come here, Quentin. What's the problem? I'm sure we can figure out a solution."

Grumbling, Quentin threw himself down on the couch. "She doesn't like me. She's the only one in the entire school who doesn't. And—you never said this was part of it—she has a boyfriend."

Veronica pursed her lush lips and arched her finely plucked eyebrows. "A boyfriend? Hmmm. You're right. That wasn't part of the equation. But things may have changed since we were last here. Our information may be dated. Well, my son, you'll just have to find a way to deal with it. One way or another."

Sabrina's head was spinning when she left the science room. What did Quentin mean, "Don't be surprised if that Harvey person doesn't ask you to the dance"? Quentin barely knew Harvey. How could he possibly stop him from asking her?

Before heading home, Sabrina swung by the Slicery, where Harvey and Jenny were already sharing a pie. She would have liked to tell them both about her confrontation with Quentin, how bordering on obnoxious he'd been, but the subject that raised his ire *was* Harvey. And the dance that he hadn't yet asked her to. It was all getting too complicated. She decided to shelve it and join her two best buds in a normal pizza-and-Foosball fest.

In fact, Quentin got pushed to the back burner of her brain all weekend. Sabrina had a ton of homework to deal with, and she'd promised to go to the mall with Jenny. Not that Sabrina ever needed to shop for clothes: When it came to conjuring up killer outfits, she'd totally mastered that wishing and pointing thing. It was her first major success using magic. She was a teenager, after all. Still, hanging at the mall with Jenny was fun. Good, clean, normal fun. Sabrina even picked up a Valentine's Day card for Harvey.

Besides, Quentin wasn't her problem. If everyone else wanted to like him, let them. If he liked her, well, she'd set him straight and that was that. And in fact, on Sunday afternoon, Harvey had actually shown up at her door, a bouquet of what could kindly be called "scraggly" flowers in his hand.

Sabrina was pumped to see him. "Hey, come in. Are those for me?"

For some reason, Harvey appeared nervous. He mumbled, "Yeah . . . I wasn't sure . . . I stopped on the way over and picked them for you. I know they're not much, but . . ."

Sabrina deftly put him out of his misery.

"They're great, Harvey, really! That was so sweet!" Sabrina took the scratchy little weeds and brought them into the kitchen, where she quickly pointed up a water-filled vase and magically added some baby's breath and dotted the "arrangement" with a few colorful daffodils. "There, now they look much better," she thought happily. When she returned to the living room, she found Harvey perched on the bottom step of the stairway that led to her room. Harvey often sat there when he wasn't sure whether to stay or go.

"So what's doing, Harvey? Want to play electronic foosball on my laptop?"

"That'd be great, Sab. But I can only stay a few minutes." Harvey explained that he'd promised to return the car to his mom—or something. Harvey wasn't always the most to-the-point person, especially when he was nervous. But he was so thoughtful, and he *was* the person whose handshake made her tingle. And whose shy smile always made her feel warm and tingly. So she sat next to Harvey on the bottom step and listened.

Eventually Harvey got around to the reason he was there. "I just wanted to make sure you were free to go to the Valentine's Day dance with me. I know I'm not the greatest dancer, but . . ."

Sabrina bounced up from the step. "Of course I'm free to go with you. Who else would I go with?"

"Ruh—uh—right," Harvey stammered as he got

up from the step and headed toward the door. "And it's not like I would go with anyone else, either. So . . . uh . . . I guess that's it. Cool! See ya in school on Monday!"

Sabrina and Harvey shook hands. She felt tingly all over.

☆

Chapter 4

☆

Where's everybody going?" Sabrina asked that of at least four people as they flew by her before homeroom on Monday morning. It seemed as if the entire school knew something she didn't. Everyone was rushing toward the gym. No one answered her until she caught up with Jenny. Her best friend stopped to tell her the news.

Breathlessly Jenny gulped, "It's Quentin. Over the weekend he got the entire archery team together. They're giving a demonstration in the gym—and announcing that they're entering the state tournament! Principal Conroy delayed first period today so everyone could attend. It's huge, Sabrina—come on!"

What? All this had happened over the weekend? She hadn't heard a thing about it. Sabrina quickened her pace to catch up with Jenny.

"How could they get good enough to enter the state tournament so fast?" Sabrina wondered out loud as she and Jenny made their way into the already packed gymnasium. "Our archery team lost to the middle school in the charity match last semester."

Jenny shrugged and searched out the rest of their friends. "Ours is not to reason why, Sabrina—ours is to find a seat and watch the arrows hit the bull's-eye!"

Sabrina couldn't even respond to that one! She let Jenny lead her to the front section of the bleachers where Harvey, Libby, Jill, Cee Cee, Larry, even Melvin and his dork contingent were perched. All the teachers were represented, too—Sabrina waved at Mr. Pool, a few rows up. He was standing next to her home ec. teacher, the acerbic Ms. Ehrenhart.

On the gym floor, over by the basketball hoop, Coach Robbins had set up a line of freestanding targets, dragged in from the playing field. The team consisted of a ragtag crew of eight boys and one girl, freckled, bespeckled Rebecca Larson. All had tried out for other teams, but none had measured up. The archery team was left; they'd take just about anyone. They were standing awkwardly on the sidelines, clutching their bows, and listening intently: Quentin was apparently giving a pep talk. He looked more like the coach than Coach. For the team and its adult leader were wearing the regulation archery uniform: gym shorts and green West-bridge tank tops over white T-shirts. Not Quentin. He had the audacity to stand out in his faded blue jeans, snug white T-shirt, and that same brown leather bomber jacket!

"I wonder if he sleeps in it," Sabrina said sarcastically.

Libby, Jenny, and even Harvey shot her an annoyed look. "Get over it, Sabrina," Libby sniffed. "He's our star player. He can *wear* whatever he *likes*. Besides, he looks hot."

Hot? He's probably stifling, Sabrina thought, easing herself out of her denim jacket. The heat in the gym was always unbearable, especially now that it was packed to the rafters.

Just then Coach Robbins and Principal Conroy walked into the center of the gym floor. Into a hand-held microphone the portly, balding school principal bellowed, "Good morning, students! Isn't it wonderful to see such an impressive turnout first thing Monday morning?

"You're all in for an exciting treat. Under the leadership of Coach Robbins, with the capable assistance of our newest transfer student . . ." As he indicated Quentin, the entire student body erupted in spontaneous applause! Haltingly Sabrina joined in. She looked around: She was by far the least enthusiastic participant.

Principal Conroy continued, ". . . Well, as I was saying, clearly you've all met Quentin. He's been classically trained in his native country, and he's quite the master archer, as we're all about to see! Anyway, our newly invigorated team will now give a demonstration of their much improved skills. The state tournament starts in a few days, and I expect after today's little preview, you'll all be there to cheer our Westbridge Archers on!"

Amid spirited applause, the principal surrendered the microphone to Coach Robbins, who summoned the team to take its positions. On the coach's cue, the first archer, a frail kid named Raymond Jackson, secured his arrow, raised his bow, pulled back tightly on the string—and let go. Ray didn't seem to have a lot of strength or speed. His arrow wobbled precariously, first dipping up slightly, then down, seemingly headed straight for the floor, several yards short of its destination. But all at once the arrow seemed to pick up steam on its own—about six inches from the ground, it righted itself and set a course straight for the bull's-eye, where it landed. Everyone cheered!

Reflexively Sabrina looked down at her own finger—had she inadvertently caused the arrow to hit the bull's-eye? But she'd folded her arms across her chest before Raymond started. No errant finger had wandered out on its own. Then Sabrina had a jolting thought—*no, not possible.*

But when the same exact same pattern occurred with the next two team members—arrows that at first seemed doomed to fall way short of the target suddenly picked up steam and hit the bull's-eye—she trained her eyes on Quentin. Was it possible?

Was he . . . *causing* the physical impossibility she was witnessing? But Quentin's fingers were all accounted for. With one hand he was gripping his own bow, waiting his turn. With the other he was holding a quiver. Naturally he was watching his teammates, grinning buoyantly, as each one succeeded in hitting the center of the target.

Quentin was up last. Sabrina had no doubt that he'd dazzle the school with his amazing ability—and he did. He also showed off. While his team members had each been limited to one shot, Quentin came up to his position with an entire quiver full of arrows. Gracefully he arched his bow—smaller than the team's, shaped slightly differently, and finely detailed, it looked like some kind of family heirloom. Theatrically he extracted one arrow at a time, positioned it, and sent it flying on its sure, graceful path to its sweet-spot destination.

After a few easy bull's-eyes, Quentin grew so cocky, he actually began shooting from different positions: He shot one arrow from over his shoulder, one with his eyes closed, another lying on his back on the gym floor!

With each bull's-eye the applause grew more fervent. It seemed the entire student body was up on its feet, cheering the deliriously joyful Mr. Pid, who took deep, dramatic bows after each shot.

Finally Quentin ran out of arrows. But that didn't stop him from arching his bow. Joyfully the school's newest hero unexpectedly swung around in circles, plucking his bow, pretending to send invisible arrows all over the gym. He seemed to seek out Sabrina and, with a wink, mimed sending one straight at her. Sabrina was not amused. Quentin kept it up for quite some time. In fact, Principal Conroy ended up canceling first period altogether.

Not surprisingly, Quentin and his show-off archery skills were the talk of the school for the rest of the day. Very little actual work got done, and even the teachers seemed swept up in the team's dramatic turnaround and the school's newest superstar. Everyone planned on attending the upcoming round-robin state archery tournaments.

Sabrina expected the entire week to be one long Quentin love-a-thon, so she was mega-surprised when it didn't turn out that way. Not that the school's spirit suddenly cooled toward the ringleted transfer student . . . just that, as the week wore on, Sabrina's classmates seemed to have other things on their minds. As in, *each* other.

It all started with Libby. By Tuesday morning the snobby cheerleader unglued herself from Quentin. That was weird all by itself. Especially when, as Sabrina found out, the two hadn't had a fight or anything. But when Libby turned the full compliment of her attentions . . . *not* to the varsity quarterback she'd been so enamored of, but to . . . Melvin Bibby? The school dork? Sabrina was flabbergasted.

Melvin was a nice enough kid, but Libby had never given him the time of day before—except to be nasty, that is. She'd had nothing but scorn for the socially-challenged boy ever since second grade! Now she seemed positively enchanted by her "Mel." She decreed his thick, prism-enhanced glasses "massively cutting edge"; his too-short pants "trendy"; and his pocket protector *"the* accessory of the millennium." She'd even taken to scribbling on her ring binder "Mrs. Libby Bibby."

Once, to teach condescending Libby a lesson, Sabrina had turned her and the entire school into dorks. But this time she was the same old Libby, still amazingly chic and awesomely stuck-up. That patented glower of hers was in full effect. She reminded everyone that Melvin was not just any random dork, he was Captain of the Dorks. And *she* had him! Weirder perhaps than all that, Melvin didn't seem surprised at Libby's sudden adoration of him. No longer intimidated by her, he actually adored her.

When Libby broke her Valentine's Day dance date with Larry, the varsity quarterback wasn't even bummed. The very next day he came to school with a bouquet of flowers, burst into archery practice, and bestowed them upon the girl previously least likely to snare his affections: the gawky Rebecca Larson. Who accepted them, *and* a Saturday night date, with a shy, knowing smile.

* * *

After school on Thursday Sabrina, Jenny, and Harvey were hanging at the Slicery, puzzling over Westbridge's newest strangest couples. Make that, Sabrina was puzzling. Jenny and Harvey didn't seem to think it was all that weird. They actually broke out in a very off-key duet of "Love Is Strange," trading off the "whoa, whoas," and slapping each other five.

In fact, all afternoon, Sabrina noticed the two of them in sync on a lot of things they'd never agreed on before. Like double pepperoni pizza. And the merits of that movie *Jerry Maguire:* Jenny had always thought it was soppy. Harvey had only liked the football scenes. Now she and Harvey decreed it the most romantic movie ever.

And then there was this sudden shared passion for pinball. Harvey and Sabrina used to compete at foosball; Jenny was never much for any game. But that Thursday afternoon there were the two of them, inches apart at the pinball machine, goofing around as they sent the beeping, pinging silver balls bouncing off the bumpers. If Sabrina didn't know better . . . *but no.*

When Sabrina had first fallen for Harvey, she wasn't alone in her crush. There had been a time— a very brief time!—when Jenny actually believed Harvey was *her* soulmate. Though Sabrina had used her magic to ferret out the truth, Jenny ended up realizing that she and Harvey were a total mismatch. Jenny had never even flirted with Harvey after that.

Until now.

Sabrina felt her confidence slipping away as she watched the two of them having the best time, blasting the machine, laughing joyously at their pinball proclivity.

But as soon as they got back to the table, Harvey slipped onto the stool next to Sabrina and offered to get her a fresh slice of pizza with her favorite topping, anchovy. He even put his arm around her when he came back with it. No, Sabrina had been way off to even think . . .

"So what do you think, Sab?" Harvey apparently had asked her a question, and Sabrina hadn't even heard it.

"Uh, what? Sorry. I zoned out," she admitted, flashing Harvey an apologetic smile.

Jenny jumped in. "Harvey was saying that he's quitting the football team to join the archery team. Isn't that *massive?*"

Massive? When did Jenny start sounding like Libby? And when did Harvey ever care about archery? "Quentin recruited me, actually," Harvey was explaining modestly. "So I figured, what the heck, I'd try it. It's not like I'll ever be a star at football. Coach benches me most of the time."

Sabrina felt Harvey's head. He must be burning up with fever or something. Harvey was crazy about football. He had worked so hard to make the team, and he'd come really far. Why would he give it up for a silly bow and arrow?

Sabrina was about to challenge Harvey's rash

decision when just then she felt someone tap her on the shoulder. She swirled around on her stool. A man in a FedEx uniform was standing next to her. "Sabrina Spellman?"

"That's . . . uh . . . me," she answered tentatively.

He produced a chunky package and a receipt. "Would you sign for this?"

All eyes in the Slicery were suddenly on Sabrina. Even the kids at the pinball machines stopped playing.

"Open it!" Jenny urged. "I'm dying to see what it is!"

"Wait!" Harvey grabbed it from her and held it to his ear. "Okay, go ahead. It's not ticking."

Sabrina had to grin. Harvey was so cute. Silly, but sweet. She tugged on the string that allowed her to rip open the package, and held it upside down. Out slipped a box; a very nice box. Of imported Belgian chocolates.

"Who's it from?" Jenny demanded as a crowd of Slicery regulars surrounded the threesome.

To the cries of "open the card," Sabrina stole a glance at Harvey. Hopeful. But his confused expression told her all she needed to know. It wasn't from him. She was barely surprised that the card was signed "Your Secret Admirer."

If it wouldn't have aroused suspicion, right at that moment Sabrina would have spirited herself away—at least down the block, where she was sure Quentin was hovering nearby. But witches are never supposed to draw attention to themselves in public. So she publicly plastered a smile across her face and stayed put, graciously inviting everyone to share in her bounty. Harvey helped himself to a handful; he didn't seem the slightest bit jealous. *But that's his nature,* Sabrina thought as she carefully put aside a few bonbons for her aunts and Salem. *Harvey's heart is true and pure. He assumes everyone else's is, too.* Only Sabrina knew differently.

The "who'd-a-thunk-it" coupling at school continued. By week's end even the teachers had entered into the romantic fray. Mr. Pool was joyously filling test tubes with jelly beans and sending them to Ms. Ehrenhart, a woman he'd previously referred to as Ms. Chilly-heart.

Principal Conroy, who'd never gotten along with Vice Principal Lautz, had taken her to dinner twice. Even intellectually challenged Coach Robbins made a play for Sabrina's brainy history teacher, Ms. Hecht. Who didn't turn him down.

"Can you believe what's going on?" Sabrina asked as she and Jenny strolled through the quad the following Monday morning on their way to homeroom. Dozens of hand-holding couples passed by them. "Libby and Melvin! Larry and Rebecca! Even Mr. Pool and Ms. Ehrenhart! I even heard Cee Cee and Jill were hanging out with Science Club members. It's like the whole school's on some wicked Love Boat or something, and you and I are, like, the only ones who stayed ashore."

It was unusual for Jenny not to instantly agree with her best friend. But this time she remained silent. Instead, the unaffected girl with the untamed hair grinned slyly. Sabrina couldn't figure out why, until Harvey sidled up to them. And slipped his hand into . . . Jenny's.

Because she was sure she would pass out if she didn't do *something,* Sabrina discretely pointed to the locked digits of her two best friends—and disentangled them.

Which didn't stop them from gazing into each other's eyes lovingly. Nor from saying the words Sabrina was sure she *wasn't* hearing. "Will you tell her, Harvey? Or should I?"

Harvey stroked Jenny's cheek "Let's tell her together, okay?"

Don't anybody tell me anything! Sabrina felt like she was shouting, but no words were coming out of her mouth. She wasn't even moving. Harvey and Jenny were easily able to guide her to their favorite bench. And tell her everything she didn't want to hear.

About how, sometime over the weekend at the archery tournament, they'd been inexplicably drawn to each other. Oh, hadn't they told Sabrina they were going to cheer on the school team? And how, somewhere between the bull's-eyes, their eyes had locked on to each other. And at exactly the same moment they suddenly discovered how much they meant to each other. Neither one wanted to hurt Sabrina. But they just couldn't help themselves: They felt all warm and tingly when they were together. So they'd spent all day Sunday deciding how they were going to break the news to her. Harvey Kinkle and Jenny Kelly were in love. And were going to the Valentine's Day dance together.

Quentin hovered behind the bushes, watching the little scene play itself out. The change in his mood was drastic. He'd started to doubt his own abilities!

But now he'd gone to Plan B, and this was looking good. Quentin could barely conceal his glee. After Harvey and Jenny left, Sabrina sat there, dazed and confused. He allowed himself the pleasure of staring at her for a while, then he dashed inside the school and over to the lockers. From his own locker he withdrew a colorful bouquet of flowers and penned an equally flowery note.

Dearest Sab, You are as beautiful and fresh as a spring bouquet. You are my destiny. Say you'll be my girlfriend.

This time he signed his real name. He wangled Sabrina's locker open and placed the bouquet inside. He glowed. Mom would be proud!

* * *

Sabrina didn't know how long she remained sitting on the bench. Faraway she thought she heard a bell ring, but she didn't have a clue what it meant. Nor did she take note of the hordes of students heading into the building to start classes. She was too shocked even to use her magic. If she had, she probably would have spirited herself away. Far away.

For the teenage witch was reeling. She'd been dumped? For Jenny? Sabrina fought hard to get a grip. She was aghast, devastated, crushed.

"Sabrina! What happened to you? Are you sick? Do you need to go to the school nurse? Sabrina . . . ?"

Words seemed to be coming at her from a thick fog. She forced herself to focus: Mr. Pool. He was standing over her, and his lips were moving. She allowed him to pierce her consciousness. "When you weren't in class this morning, I went to the office to see if you were absent. When I found you had gone to homeroom, I asked if anyone knew where you were. Quentin mentioned he'd seen you out here. Sabrina . . . you look strange. Is there anything I can do?"

Mr. Pool's solid presence jolted her back to reality. In a flash she came to her senses.

Harvey and Jenny? No way! Sabrina didn't know exactly what was really going on, but she suddenly and most assuredly knew this: Quentin Pid had something to do with it. And she was not ready to surrender. Not her boyfriend *or* her best friend. And certainly not to each other!

Thanking Mr. Pool for his concern, and assuring him she was fine, she bolted up and dashed to her locker to gather her books. Sabrina tossed the bouquet of flowers in the nearest trash bin. She didn't bother to read the card.

Chapter 5

This is *so* not happening!" Sabrina was fuming. Lightning and thunderbolts rocked the neighborhood. She'd plowed through the rest of the school day fueled by fury and a determination to stop the insanity. But so far no plan had presented itself. And when frustrated witches rage, the weather patterns in the neighborhood feel it.

"Calm down, Sabrina," levelheaded Aunt Zelda entreated her as she blasted through the door after school. "You're going to drown all the plants. Come into the kitchen and tell us what's going on."

"Enough with the waterworks," Salem added, trailing them, "or get me another feline, and I'll gladly march two by two into the ark."

But Sabrina was livid. Nothing—nothing!— could calm her down. She stomped around the kitchen, pointing her finger skyward. With each point another thunderclap shook the house.

"I *know* Quentin had something to do with this! I don't know how, and I don't know what—but . . ." Suddenly her eyes flew open and she sprung over to her aunts. She demanded, "Is this a test? Because if it is, you know, I've really had enough. I've passed everything you've thrown at me, and besides, you're always picking on me and Harvey. . . ."

"It's not a test! It's not a test!" Hilda had to shout to be heard above Sabrina's roar. "But if you don't chill out, I'm going to have to test that new freeze-dried recipe on you . . . *capice?*"

Sabrina understood. Her aunts *did* have their ways of calming her down. Casting a spell and bringing her to a screeching halt as it were.

"Okay," Hilda said when Sabrina finally stopped ranting and pointing, "Now, *sit.* Take deep calming breaths. Have some ice cream." Hilda pointed at the freezer, which magically opened. A quart of Rocky Road floated toward Sabrina and gently glided onto the table in front of her. Zelda pointed to the silverware drawer: a spoon drifted over.

After Hilda secured a spoon for herself, explaining that she could feel Sabrina's pain much more thoroughly this way, the aunts convinced their niece to explain the crisis du jour.

Sabrina dug into the quart with such vengeance, she bent the spoon. "It's Quentin! That jerk from the movies! He broke us up! Now Harvey's going out with Jenny! And the brat claims to be in love with me!"

Zelda stood over Sabrina, hands on her hips. She shook her head. "Not possible, Sabrina. No one but you and Harvey have any power over your relationship."

Salem, licking the ice cream from the open lid, offered, "Maybe Jenny and Harvey can't help themselves: It's animal attraction." Sabrina thought she'd swat the cat.

"Salem has a point, Sabrina," Hilda said a little too enthusiastically. "Two centuries ago, Drell broke our date to go out with some babe named Amonia, saying it was a chemical attraction."

Salem snickered. "So let's recap here. The love of Sabrina's life dumped her. The jerk Sabrina doesn't like, on the other paw, is after her. Now I remember why those seven hundred years of being a teenager were pure agony!"

Thoughtfully Zelda added, "All sorts of weird things happen to mortals when spring is in the air."

Sabrina scoffed. "Spring? It's February! The only thing in the air *and* on the ground is Quentin Pid. He did something! I know it! He said something to Harvey! I don't know what he did to turn Harvey against me. But I *am* going to get to the bottom of this. By any means necessary."

"What happens when you do, Sabrina? What if you find out that Quentin isn't responsible for Harvey's change of heart? Then how will you feel?"

Aunt Zelda was always trying to get her to consider the consequences before she rashly took action.

Sabrina considered them. "How will I feel when I know the truth? No worse than I feel now."

Sabrina pushed herself away from the table, leaving Hilda and Salem to polish off the ice cream. Morosely she trudged upstairs. But not before Zelda cautioned, "Whatever you do, Sabrina, forget love spells. You can't make someone fall in love with you . . . or make someone else fall out of love with you. Not by magic."

Yes, Sabrina knew. In matters of the heart, mortals and witches had to follow the same rules, and magic was not part of the equation. But *something* was going on here. Nothing could convince her that Harvey and Jenny "suddenly discovered" some long-buried mutual attraction.

Sabrina paced her room, hoping a solution would present itself. Hoping against hope the phone would ring, and it would be Harvey, who suddenly came to his senses and realized Sab was his girlfriend. And of course *they* were going to the dance together. "Who else would I go with, Sab?" Those were the words she longed to hear.

She even put a spell on the phone. *"In the next two minutes you will ring, good news from Harvey you will bring!"* But every time the phone rang it was some other Harvey—not her Harvey—seized with the uncontrollable urge to share some wonderful news with someone named Sabrina.

* * *

Sabrina slept fitfully, but she barely ruffled the sheets on her bed. Instead, the conflicted young witch spent the night floating all over the room. When she woke, she wasn't even near her bed, but splayed atop her dresser, arms and legs bent over the piece of furniture.

She was bent for something else, too: revenge. Not against Harvey or Jenny, whom she considered innocent pawns in some bizarre game. No, she was going to make Quentin Pid sorry he'd transferred into her life and messed it up.

As Sabrina pointed up a killer outfit of boot cut hip-huggers and a satin shirt, she confided only in Salem. Of everyone in her household, the cat best understood revenge. "I know I'm not supposed to use magic on defenseless mortals—but if anyone deserves it, Quentin Pid does!"

"You go, witch!" Salem egged her on, licking his chops. "I only wish I could be there to revel in the devastation!"

Determined to wage war on Quentin Pid, Sabrina wasted no time, but approached her erstwhile suitor first thing at the lockers. His back was to her—he was still wearing that unbearable jacket. Sabrina tapped him on the shoulder. Quentin spun around. He nearly blinded her with his high-beam smile. He was so resplendent, she was momentarily unnerved. "I hope you liked the flowers, Sab. And the candy. By now I guess you figured out they were from me."

His use of Harvey's pet name for her jolted her into action. "I asked you please not to call me that, Quentin." Sabrina looked straight into Quentin's unclouded, ice-blue eyes. She raised her finger right between them.

She pointed. He didn't blink, but gazed at her adoringly.

She shot. A bolt of magic headed straight for its bull's-eye. He still didn't blink.

She . . .

. . . did not score.

The huge ugly zit that should have transformed him from handsome to horrid did not appear. Instead, his smooth, luminescent skin remained radiant, completely clear. "What's the matter, Sab?" Quentin actually seemed concerned. "You look really weirded out."

What happened? Why did my magic fail me? Slowly Sabrina circled Quentin. *Maybe because I slept funny last night, the zit's on his back—or somewhere else?* But Quentin appeared undamaged. Minty fresh—and blemish-free.

"I have an idea," he suddenly said as if trying to cheer her up. "Why not come to the archery tournament this afternoon? As my guest. We're playing our biggest rivals, Eastwick High. It's on our athletic field after last period. If we win this, we've captured the county title, and we're a lock for the state tournament. We have a lot of fans, but I'll save a front row seat for you. How 'bout it?"

Sabrina was about to tell him she had better things to do than sit around mooning over him at an archery game—a root canal would be preferable. Still, she realized, attending the game meant another magical shot at him. This one in front of his "fans." This one would not fail.

Sabrina had never thought of herself as a spiteful person, but right now she was angry, frustrated, and boyfriend-challenged. All of which she attributed to the angel-faced would-be boyfriend standing right in front of her. She agreed to meet him later.

As Sabrina dashed down the corridor to homeroom, Quentin shouted after her, "See you later. You won't be sorry you came, Sab."

You might, thought Sab.

Sabrina's mood did not improve as the day wore on. How could it? Everywhere she turned, disparate loving couples were swooning all over each other. In science class Mr. Pool made the mysteries of mytosis sound like a romance novel. In home ec., Ms. Ehrenhart had them bake heart-shaped cookies. Ms. Hecht devised a lesson about the heroic history of archery—weaving her newly beloved Coach Robbins into the narrative.

And Principal Conroy and Vice Principal Lautz together decreed "no homework" Tuesday, so everyone could enjoy the archery tournament without the "burden" of homework to deal with.

* * *

Later, Sabrina found that Quentin had indeed earmarked a seat for her, in the front row of the bleachers. She was next to Larry Carson, there to cheer his beloved Rebecca on. All around her were girls who were dating other members of the team. Including Jenny. Sabrina's best friend could barely conceal her joy when the game began and Harvey, looking hot in his Westbridge Archers uniform, stepped up to his mark. Sabrina could barely conceal her pain.

Harvey wasn't the only new team member. In fact, several players had deserted the school's other sports teams to join.

Naturally, the cheerleaders, led by the future Mrs. Melvin Bibby—Libby, that is—had switched their allegiance. No longer did the popular girls rah-rah the football team. Their siss-boom-bahs were now exclusive to the archery team.

And the mighty Archers routinely dispatched their competitors. They were easily on their way to the state championships. Before Quentin's arrival, the team had been little more than a joke. Now its members were school superstars.

Well, that's cool. Let them be superstars, Sabrina thought. *They deserve it. All but Quentin, that is.* For him, Sabrina had a plan. For which he'd need that trademark jacket. He might be a little cold soon. As in, freezing.

Freezing people was a handy little trick she'd learned some months ago. It worked sort of like the pause button on the VCR: stopping the action momentarily, rendering one's subject frozen in place. The moment lasted as long as Sabrina deemed necessary. Freezing magic was not a tactic the teenage witch employed often. It wasn't nice to interfere with mortals, especially innocent ones. But she was sure Quentin didn't fall into the innocent part of that category.

Sabrina's plan was to freeze him just at the moment he was poised to take his best shot. Then she'd take hers. To his adoring fans, it would seem that Quentin had inexplicably choked. By the time she unfroze him—say five or ten minutes later— the time limit for his turn would expire. He'd have to forfeit.

Quentin was up last. Raymond Jackson scored effortlessly, as did the blushing Rebecca Larson— cheered on vociferously by Larry Carson. Each team member took a shot against an Eastwick competitor, and each time the result was the same: the Westbridge Archers were closer to the bull's-eye. When Harvey came up, Sabrina determined to cheer louder than Jenny. Although she felt badly about it, she mischievously froze Jenny's vocal chords, so her best friend couldn't possibly out-cheer her.

And then it was Quentin's turn. The crowd roared for its newest hero. Even the Eastwick girls seemed enamored of Quentin. The ringleted charmer was loving every minute of it, theatrically strutting to his mark.

Love this, Sabrina thought.

Quentin took his stance.

Sabrina stood up and took hers.

Quentin secured his arrow and pulled back on the string.

Sabrina muttered an incantation: *"Bend your bow, take your aim, you will freeze, with no one but yourself to blame."*

Quentin closed one eye and aimed.

Sabrina kept both of hers open and pointed.

The second Quentin went to release his arrow, both he and Sabrina were beaming victoriously. A microsecond later the upturned corners of Sabrina's mouth drooped dangerously downward.

For just like the zit that wasn't, her freeze frame completely fizzled. Once again Sabrina's magic had failed her. Her plan tanked; his ranked. For just as *he'd* planned it, Quentin's arrow whizzed through the air, arched gracefully, and came to rest at its final destination. Bull's-eye.

The crowd was up on its feet, cheering wildly. Not only had Westbridge handily won the game, they'd done it decisively. A stunning upset, thanks mostly to Quentin Pid.

Principal Conroy dashed onto the field. He waited until the cheering subsided. Then he shouted into his hand-held microphone, "I have two important announcements. The first will come as no surprise. Because of our exemplary showing today, beating our worthy opponents at Eastwick for the county title, our very own Westbridge Archers have secured a spot in the state championship tournament, which begins next week."

"And, to further give us something to cheer about, I've just received word that a consortium of state businesses has pledged a sizable donation to the school with the winning archery team. If our team wins, we can put it toward an entire new athletic field!"

Principal Conroy ended his speech by extending a special thanks to the student who single-handedly turned the Archers around. "Greece's loss is Westbridge's gain!"

The conquering hero basked in his glory, barely acknowledging the rest of the team. But he did seek out one person in the stands. As his teammates filed back into the lockers to change and celebrate, he strode up to Sabrina. She was still standing, completely shocked. Egocentric Quentin assumed her astonished expression was one of awe, for him.

He took her hand in his. Sabrina swiftly withdrew it, but Quentin wasn't deterred. Adoringly he whispered, "I'm glad you decided to come, Sab. You *inspired* me to greatness."

Sabrina was inspired to gag. Just then Harvey came loping over to the grandstand. For a moment she was sure he was coming to tell her the whole thing with Jenny had been a joke. But Harvey looked right past her—into Jenny's eyes. "Harvey! You were amazing, brilliant," Jenny cooed.

Sabrina felt a hot rush of anger. If magic didn't work . . . maybe good old-fashioned jealousy would. Impulsively she grabbed Quentin's hand and, making sure Harvey could see, proclaimed loudly, "I'm so proud of you, Quentin. Like Principal Conroy said, you turned this team around."

But instead of being jolted to his senses, all Harvey said was, "Hey, you two want to join us at the Slicery? The four of us could split a large pizza."

Recklessly Sabrina blurted out, "We'd love to! Wouldn't we, Quentin? Only make our half anchovies. That's Quentin's favorite!" If Harvey noticed the sarcasm in her voice, he didn't show it.

As he and Harvey strode back to the lockers, Quentin was beside himself with joy. It was working! Sabrina, his Sabrina, was falling for him. How could he have doubted his own abilities? It had been an excellent idea to get Harvey out of the way, and then to become a school hero. So what if he hadn't exactly played fair to accomplish his goal? Fairness, in his mind, was overrated. Had been for centuries. Besides, his family had invented a special expression: All's fair in love and war. To Quentin, this was both.

"This is pretty neat, huh? We aced the counties, we're in the state tournament, and we've got our best girls waiting for us after the game. It doesn't get any better than this." Harvey's voice jolted Quentin out of his joyful reverie.

As Harvey sauntered toward his locker, Quentin ducked around to the other side of the room. He never, *ever* changed in front of anyone.

Less than a half hour later Sabrina found herself squeezed in between Harvey and Quentin, perched on a stool at a center table in the Slicery. Ordinarily, being this close to Harvey made her heart sing, but this was hardly an ordinary afternoon. Especially since Harvey and Jenny were ever so cutely sharing the same slice of pizza. Balancing it on their fingertips, Harvey was chewing from the crusty end, while Jenny was simultaneously nibbling at the tip. They were giggling in between bites. Harvey thought it was especially cute when the cheese stuck to Jenny's nose. He nibbled it off.

Okay, this is it. Maybe the zit didn't happen, and maybe my aim was off on the archery field, but this time, I am getting to the bottom of this. For Sabrina had set off that morning with one more piece of ammunition: truth sprinkles. When ingested by anyone—witches or mortals—that person was impelled to say exactly what was really on his or her mind.

She'd tucked the little bottle in her backpack. Now, surreptitiously, she fished it out. With a discreet flick of her wrist Sabrina dusted the tiny sprinkles on Harvey's half of the pizza, and silently chanted, *"Sprinkle, sprinkle, Harvey Kinkle, on the one you* truly *love, your eyes will twinkle."*

As Harvey bit into the slice, Sabrina remembered Aunt Zelda's warning: "The truth may hurt, Sabrina. You may not really want to hear it." But Sabrina didn't think she could hurt anymore than she already did, watching her boyfriend nibble cheese off her best friend's nose.

She was wrong.

For just as Sabrina finished her chant, and Harvey swallowed, he flashed his hazel eyes on the one he truly loved: Jenny Kelly. And it hurt worse than anything had before.

Frustrated, Sabrina less discreetly gave Jenny's half of the slice a dousing, blurting out, "Jenny! Tell me the truth! Why are you stealing Harvey? Who put you up to this?"

Jenny ate her pizza, then abruptly tore herself away from Harvey's gaze to face Sabrina. With a bright innocent smile she said, "No one put me up to this, Sabrina. Harvey and I just can't help the way we feel for each other."

Sabrina spun around in her stool. "Maybe you can't help it, but I bet you had some help." With that, she recklessly tossed the contents of the rest of the bottle into Quentin's soda. Impatiently she waited until he downed it. Then Sabrina hissed, "The truth, Quentin! I want it now! What did you tell Harvey to make him dump me for Jenny?"

Instead of being shocked or annoyed, Quentin

was charmed. With a backward toss of his golden ringlets, he laughed. "You are so cute when you're mad, Sabrina. I'm crazy about you." That he found Sabrina's uncouth behavior amusing shouldn't have surprised her. Throwing food in a public place, after all, was right up his alley.

But when Quentin added, "No one told me you'd be *this* cute," a little red flag went up in Sabrina's brain. Suspiciously she demanded, "Who told you anything about me?"

Quickly Quentin covered up. "No one, just an expression, that's all. Look, Sab, we've hardly had a chance to spend any time alone. How about going out with me on Friday night?"

Sabrina turned to check out Harvey and Jenny. The love couple were on their second shared slice. Sabrina felt her heart breaking in two.

All at once she felt a gentle hand on her chin. Quentin. Sabrina allowed him to turn her away from Harvey and Jenny.

For the first time Sabrina tried to see him in a different light. He really was cute. He really liked her. Maybe, in her heartache over Harvey falling for Jenny, she'd totally misjudged the whole situation. Maybe Quentin just had a really intense crush on her. Maybe his appalling behavior at the movies was an aberration. Maybe he was worth getting to know. So many *maybes.*

Including this one: If she *did* go on a date with him, the opportunity to kiss him might come up.

And if it did, since she didn't love him and they weren't friends, her kiss just might turn him into a frog. And if it did—that is, if her magic worked this time—she'd be rid of Quentin Pid forever.

"What do you say, Sab? We could go to the movies. It'll be fun."

Sabrina made her decision. "I say . . . sure! It could be more fun than you know." Under her breath she croaked, "R-r-r-ibbit!"

Chapter 6

☆

☆

Sabrina spent the remainder of the week obsessed with Quentin Pid. Why hadn't her magic worked on him? She spent hours poring over *The Discovery of Magic,* the spell book she'd been given for her sixteenth birthday. It overflowed with helpful hints, incantations, and instructions for using her powers. Nowhere could she find the answer she was looking for.

Her aunts didn't have it, either—although Sabrina was never totally sure if Hilda, Zelda, and even Salem really didn't know stuff, or they just believed she should figure it out for herself. After a few days the best Sabrina could come up with was that her magic hadn't worked on Quentin because she'd been cranky when she tried to give him a zit, and her aim was off on the archery field. She tried to squelch the other possibility, the one the truth sprinkles suggested: *I'm not that good at my magic, and Harvey and Jenny really are in love.*

Sabrina slammed the book shut. She would not accept any of it.

Besides, she would not goof up on Friday night. She'd get a lot of rest on Thursday, and her aim— straight for Quentin's lips—would be nothing but bull's-eye. One peck from her, and it was shooting arrows from the backs of floating lily pads for him. *Rrr-rr-i-bit!*

Quentin spent the remainder of the week obsessed with himself. He really, really liked high school here. Not that he fit in: even better, he stood out. He was in the spotlight, and deservedly so.

Besides, it wasn't as if he had to actually *work* in school. His teachers, drawn to his charm as much as they were to each other these days, let him slide by. He never did homework, spoke up in class only to interrupt, shot paper airplanes around the room, and cheated on tests.

In the cafeteria Quentin-instigated food fights were now a daily occurrence. He didn't care about the losers who got blamed for his misdeeds and had to stay and clean it all up. These kids were so easily manipulated!

All but one, that is. Sabrina Spellman: the one who would be his date Friday night, and for the Valentine's Day dance, and then, come back home with him. The whole wooing process was taking a lot longer than anticipated. That girl had somehow managed to dodge his advances and resist his charm. Even after he'd gotten that Harvey dolt out of the way.

But this Friday he'd go on a date with her. A date Quentin had special plans for. Sabrina would fall for him on that date, he'd make sure of it. He'd be so close to her, he couldn't miss. His aim would be true.

Sabrina didn't normally hide things from her family, but she conveniently neglected to tell Hilda, Zelda, and even Salem of her plan to afflict Quentin with amphibian-itis. She knew they'd disapprove. Aunt Zelda would probably say, "Just because you're angry at him is no reason to turn him into a frog." And then Aunt Hilda would probably go into some convoluted story about the time she tried to turn Napoleon or King Arthur or Christopher Columbus into a frog and how it backfired. And then Salem would . . .

"Sabrina! Can we come in?"

Her aunts and Salem were at her bedroom door. Sabrina checked the time. Quentin would arrive momentarily. She'd been holed up in her room for the past hour, pointing up dozens of potential date outfits. She'd finally gone with a green theme— might as well match her date, she thought mischievously—and settled on lime-green hip-huggers paired with a forest green checked shiny shirt. Her nail polish was actually called "Tricky Green."

"Enter at your own risk," Sabrina called out to

them. But when Zelda and Hilda stepped in, they didn't notice the outfit. By the expressions on their faces, Sabrina knew instantly they suspected something.

"Not that we want to rush to judgment, Sabrina, but your agreeing to a date with Quentin seems awfully sudden, especially since you've spent the last few weeks so angry at him, we nearly needed to build a moat around the house," Aunt Zelda began.

"And especially since you waited until the last minute even to tell us about it," Hilda continued.

"Not to mention you didn't even confide in me. And I rule on the subject of revenge," Salem scoffed, offended at being left out of the loop.

"Revenge? Who said anything about revenge?" Sabrina tried to keep her tone casual as she fibbed, "I'm just testing the waters. It's possible you were right, and Quentin is okay. After tonight I'll know for sure."

Three pairs of eyes stared at her—two witches, one feline—not believing. The doorbell saved Sabrina from having to elaborate. As she dashed past her aunts, she pleaded, "Could you guys do me one favor and stay upstairs? I'm not real comfortable with you meeting him. Yet."

Sabrina didn't get an argument, just a dab of last-minute advice. "Don't do anything I wouldn't do," Hilda reminded her. "Don't let him find out you're not exactly mortal."

Sabrina stopped short of the door, and spun around to glance up at her aunts, poised parentally at the top of the stairs. She grinned at them. "Don't worry. I'm not wearing my button that says, 'I'm A Witch! Ask Me How.'"

Brimming with confidence, the teenage witch flung the door open. That's when she nearly fell over: Quentin looked amazing. Double amazing. More amazing than ever. The baseball cap was gone, and his golden curls glistened in the moonlight, shining almost as brightly as his 1000-watt smile.

Sartorially, Quentin had pulled out all the stops. He'd switched from jeans to pressed khakis, into which he'd tucked a denim button-down shirt. Over it, and most incredible of all, was a tweed sports jacket. It was the first time Sabrina had seen him without the leather bomber jacket. He had another accessory: a delicate bunch of blushing-pink baby roses. "For you, Sab. May I come in?"

Sabrina finally caught her breath. "These are . . . you look . . . I mean . . . *wow,*" she stammered, stepping aside to let Quentin in the house. She stammered, "Uh, I'll just put you, I mean, them, the flowers, that is, in a vase. Wait here. I mean, come in. I mean, duh, you *are* in. I'll be right back."

Sabrina blushed. She was truly flustered. She hadn't expected Quentin to look so . . . *amazingly* cute. Sabrina pulled herself together and dashed to the kitchen, where she pointed up a vase—the same one that had held Harvey's flowers only a few weeks ago—and then returned to the living room.

Her aunts, she noticed with relief, had respected

her wishes and not come down. But Salem had. He'd engaged Quentin in a staring contest. Which Sabrina knew was no contest: The cat would win, paws down.

"Cute cat," Quentin said as Sabrina hustled him out the door. "Sorry I didn't get to meet the rest of your family. Maybe next time."

Like there'll be a next time? Only if I channel Miss Piggy! Sabrina pictured the Kermit-like Quentin she'd be rendering a few hours hence. Then she actually caught herself thinking what a shame that would be: *he is too cute for words. Oh, well, he'll make a cute frog, that's all.*

Quentin led her to his car, parked behind Zelda's in the driveway. That was Sabrina's second shock of the evening: her dashing date drove . . . a shocking pink Volkswagen Beetle? "I haven't seen one of these in ages!" she exclaimed. "And definitely not in this color."

Quentin beamed, proud of his wheels. "I had it shipped from Greece." Then, like a perfect gentleman, he held the door open for her. As Sabrina slid into the bucket seat, she noticed his archery case in the back. "Never leave home without it, huh?" she quipped as Quentin settled behind the wheel and turned the motor on.

"An archer's day is never done, you know, Sab? And you never know when you'll find a handy target to practice on."

Odd response. Unless he was planning to take her to a shooting range for their date. But as he backed out of the driveway, he suggested, "I thought we'd go to the movies. Is that okay with you?"

Sabrina nodded and strapped the seat belt on. Tentatively she ventured, "Look, Quentin, could I ask you a question?"

"Anything, Sab! Fire away. I'm all yours."

All mine? When frogs fly, Quentin, Sabrina thought. *All I want is to get back with Harvey, which seems to mean getting* you *out of the way.*

"Um, okay, I know this might sound weird, but what's up with that jacket of yours? I mean, the one you wear every day, even for archery. Aren't you . . . I don't know . . . hot or something?"

Quentin seemed startled and braked a little too hard at the traffic light. "My jacket? That's what you want to know about? All right, well, I guess it's what you might call my lucky jacket."

Sabrina considered. "You didn't need luck tonight?"

Quentin didn't take his eyes off the road. "My luck was getting you to go out with me." The light changed, and they drove in silence for a while. Sabrina thought Quentin might ask her about herself, but when he finally spoke again, it was to inquire, "So what else do you want to know about me, my sweet Sab?"

She bristled. "Could you really not call me that, Quentin? I told you. It's kind of a special name my boyfriend uses."

When Quentin stopped for the next red light, he

gazed at Sabrina. Softly he said, "I was hoping you were over him, and that I could be your boyfriend."

Sabrina sighed. He wasn't giving up. Neither was she.

Of the six possibilities at the Westbridge multiplex, Quentin suggested one Harvey never would have: a romantic comedy. Sabrina would have liked to see it. In fact, she reflected, under other circumstances, this would have been a perfect night. She looked great; she was out with a cute, popular sports hero; and, best of all, she was doing something completely normal, a Friday night movie date. Only without Harvey? Everything about this was totally wrong!

Sabrina turned her nose up and opted for the film Harvey *would* have chosen: a Jackie Chan actioner.

Quentin didn't quibble with her choice, just expressed surprise. "Usually, girls prefer more romantic movies."

"What can I say? I'm an unusual girl," Sabrina responded brightly.

With great seriousness Quentin agreed. "That you are, Sab."

At the candy counter he surprised her by not loading up on tons of sweets, like that first time she'd seen him. After treating Sabrina to a giant box of Milk Duds, he ordered a small unbuttered popcorn and a Coke for himself. Just to be safe, Sabrina elected to keep her jacket on: in case

Quentin felt the sudden urge to start a food fight. His childish side *had* begun to show in school lately—not that anyone but her seemed to care.

But the loutish side of Quentin was well under wraps that night. He only annoyed her once, trying to put his arm around her. Sabrina squiggled, letting him know she wasn't cool with it. He got the message.

After the movie Quentin asked her where she wanted to go. Sabrina was hungry, and if he were Harvey, she'd have suggested an ice cream parlor, deli, the Slicery even. But he wasn't, and she didn't.

"Home, I guess," she replied. Why prolong the night? He'd definitely try for a kiss before she got out of the car. And she'd most definitely let him. In fact, if he didn't go for it, she would.

"Home it is, then," Quentin responded. He didn't sound disappointed.

Twenty minutes later the twosome pulled up in Sabrina's driveway. Zelda's car was still there. Sabrina hoped Quentin wouldn't ask to come in and meet her family. But he made no mention of it, nor was he in any hurry, after he turned off the motor, to get out of the car. In fact, the first thing he did was unbuckle the seat belt so he could lean over and grab his archery case and quiver.

Sabrina arched her eyebrows. "You see a target in sight, Quentin?"

Quentin deftly removed the latch and opened the case. "I thought you might want a close-up view of my bow. And arrows. They're kind of made-to-order."

Sabrina wasn't particularly interested, never had been, but she wanted to seem super attentive tonight. She peered into the case as he lifted the bow out. And he was right, his archery equipment *was* different from any she'd ever seen. The bow was half the size of the ones the team used, and intricately designed. "It's pretty," she ventured, running her finger along the carved etchings. "I guess it's lucky for you, like your jacket."

"It's more like a part of me," he answered as he pretended to withdraw an arrow from the quiver and secure it in the bow. Sabrina watched intently as Quentin closed one eye, mimed pulling the string back and—inches from her face—he pretended to shoot an arrow at her.

Since his arrow was virtual, she didn't flinch. Her rapt expression remained exactly the same.

That's when Quentin unexpectedly recoiled. All of a sudden he seemed disoriented, flustered. He stammered, much as she had hours earlier. "I don't understand," he mumbled. "Sabrina—don't you . . . feel . . . anything?"

He really is weird. Sabrina, nevertheless, was determined to carry out her plan. As the flummoxed Quentin furrowed his brow and set his bow and arrow down on his lap, Sabrina gulped and whispered nervously, "You know, I do feel something, Quentin. I feel like . . ."

Could she really do this? She pictured Harvey.

". . . uh, kissing you."

Quentin lit up. "You do? That's wonderful! It worked! I mean, by your expression just then, I never would have known."

Quentin was overjoyed, but strangely made no move toward her. It was up to Sabrina. Shaking, she removed the bow and arrow from his lap and slid them on the floor. Leaning in toward Quentin, she gently placed one hand on his shoulder. She crossed the fingers of her other hand behind her back—hoping it would have the same effect as when you know you're telling a lie. Then she closed her eyes and puckered her lips. As she felt them graze his, she silently chanted, *"With this kiss, I decree, one hundred years as a frog you'll be."*

As Sabrina kissed Quentin, she felt two things: the softness of his full lips, mixed with the icky reality that this was definitely not Harvey. No matter what her goal, and no matter who Harvey was with tonight, for her, locking lips with Quentin felt like cheating.

For a split second she almost forgot what she *didn't* feel—anything remotely slimy, wet, and/or scaly. Or any combination of the above.

Quentin, on the other hand, was ecstatic. Instead of croaking some low-decibel variation of "rr-rribbit," or breaking into a chorus of "It's Not Easy Being Green," his eyes remained closed, his lips parted just slightly, and he was murmuring something truly weird. It sounded like "At last, my beloved Psyche . . ."

Startled, Sabrina abruptly pulled away. *"Psyche* is right! You *didn't* turn into a frog!!"

Quentin's huge, clear blue eyes opened slowly, dreamily. Through long, lush lashes, he peered at her. "Why would I, my love? My destiny?"

All at once Sabrina's head was pounding. She felt all too mortal, morti*fied* even. "I have a headache, Quentin. I'm going in." She bolted out of the car and up the driveway. She didn't bother to thank him for a . . . lovely, albeit, frog-challenged evening.

Sabrina flew into the house, flinging the front door open with such force, it almost came unhinged. And that's when it hit her like the bolts of lightning and thunderclaps she was causing with her furious thrusting digit.

She shrieked, "He's a *warlock!* That's *it!* I can't believe I didn't think of this before! I am *such* a jerk!" Her shouts rose above the raging storms and brought Zelda, Hilda, and Salem careening down the steps.

They had to whip up an entire cauldron of Calm-Down soup—to get Sabrina relaxed and settled on the couch. But after a few seconds of composure, she'd jump up and start in again, ranting and raving.

"Don't you get it? He ruined my life, so I tried everything on him, and nothing worked! He's got to be . . ."

Hilda, wearing her favorite tattered flannel twelfth-century nightgown, was nonplussed. "I hope you didn't try a revenge zit. I tried that during the Crusades, but all I did was give Richard the Lion Hearted a really bad skin day. Which caused him to be really mean when he stomped through Greenland . . ."

"The zit didn't work!" Sabrina seethed. "I couldn't freeze him, the truth sprinkles made him giggle—giggle!—like an insane hyena!" Sabrina paced the living room frantically. "Worst of all," she moaned, "I forced myself to kiss him . . . and he didn't even croak. And I've got the hang of this witch thing by now—my magic works on everybody. Everybody but him. Coincidence? I think *not!*"

If it all seemed crystal clear to Sabrina, it was still extremely blurry to her aunts. Zelda, wrapped in her this-century chenille robe, tried level-headed reasoning. "It's highly improbable that Quentin and his family are visiting from the Other Realm. If they were, we'd know about it. We're a small community. Word would get out."

"She's right," Hilda agreed, "There's almost no one we don't know, or are in some way related to. There's only six degrees of separation among witch families. We've even got our own version of that Kevin Bacon game. It's called the Six Degrees of Samantha. I'll give you an example. See if you can connect Glinda, the good witch of the east, with

Samantha from *Bewitched*. I'll give you a hint. It has to do with the Tin Man, Ozzie Osbourne, and Darrin. But the second Darrin . . ."

Sabrina was not in the mood for games. She'd already tuned her aunts out. She kept jumping up from the couch, pacing the living room, shaking her head violently. She couldn't *believe* she'd been so blind. Of course her magic hadn't worked on him: Quentin had his own magic to repel hers!

The whole scenario reminded her of the time her jealous cousin Tanya had visited. Tanya had avoided Sabrina's magic using an invisible shield. Whatever spells Sabrina flung on Tanya boomeranged back onto her. Sabrina had to learn to create her own shield in self-defense.

Not that Quentin was doing that. But he was doing something worse: casting misguided love spells all over her school. Didn't he know that terrible things happen when you meddle in the lives of mortals? Besides, he had to know that love spells rarely work on mortals, and couldn't possibly work on her anyway. He already knew she was a witch. Hadn't he once even said, "Sabrina Spellman, you've put a spell on me?"

Salem perched on the armrest of the couch, watching Sabrina go ballistic, while Hilda and Zelda tried to reason with her. The cat twitched his whiskers. "I don't know what you're so wigged about, Sabrina. Being a warlock makes Quentin a much better catch than that tongue-tied Harvey— the Wizard of 'Uhs.'"

Hilda admitted with a giggle, "I sneaked a peek from my bedroom window when you two were in the car—Quentin *is* kind of cute."

Sabrina stopped in her tracks and emitted a long, exasperated sigh. Her aunts were totally not getting this. In the most reasonable voice she could summon, she said, "It's not just that Quentin cast some kind of spell and made Harvey fall for Jenny, he's turned the whole school upside down. Teachers are so in love with each other they're not teaching! And I just know he used his magic to ace those archery tournaments and steal victories from other schools' deserving teams. Aren't you the ones who taught me that magic isn't supposed to be used recklessly against defenseless mortals—or for ill gain?"

Sabrina's aunts couldn't disagree with that. But they could cast doubts on her conclusion.

Zelda insisted, "All right, your magic didn't work on him. And if he *was* mortal, a first kiss from you should have turned him into a frog. But I still think if a witch family came to town, Hilda and I would know. We still head up the Witches' Welcome Wagon around here."

It was Hilda who came up with a plan. "I say we give Sabrina the benefit of the doubt—and the benefit of our wisdom. If Quentin is a warlock, that means at least one of his parents is, too. So let's get an up-close view of them. Two more experienced witches will know right away—"

"Two more experienced witches? What I am, chopped Kibbles 'N Bits?" Salem sniffed.

Hilda amended, "Okay, two more experienced witches and the warlock formerly known as Salem Saberhagen. Sabrina, call Quentin up now and invite his family to dinner tomorrow night. Once we get the Pid pod on our turf, we'll get some real answers."

Sabrina allowed herself to feel hopeful. She threw her arms around Hilda. "Cool! The sooner we get to the bottom of this, the sooner I get Harvey back."

As she picked up the phone and punched in Quentin's number, she tried to ignore Salem's singsong, tail-waving teasing, "Harvey Loves Jenny, Quentin Loves Sabrina."

After she'd spoken to Quentin, she impulsively punched in Harvey's number. He wasn't home, so she left a sweet message on his answering machine. He may have forgotten her, but she'd never forget him.

☆

Chapter 7

☆

Quentin tingled with joy. Although he was behind the wheel of his car, he felt as if he floated all the way home. On the wings of love, as it were.

"She loves me! Yeah, yeah, yeah! She loves me, yeah, yeah, yeah, *yeah!*" Quentin was still singing at the top of his lungs as he danced through the door of his home. He was so loud and off-key, he woke his mom, who'd dozed off on the couch, and his dad, who came stomping out of the bedroom.

Martin Pid was not amused. "Never liked the Beatles," he thundered, irritated at his son's sappy mood. "Stop with the 'All you need is love' line and give us cold, hard facts."

Quentin often got annoyed at his dad, but not tonight. Nothing could spoil this moment. For his plan had worked, Sabrina was his. She kissed him!

He felt the thrill of victory coursing through his veins as he explained the events of the past few hours to his parents. He didn't bother mentioning that strange frog comment Sabrina had made.

As expected, his mom beamed with pride. She came over and hugged him. "I knew you could do it, my son. When will you be bringing her to me?"

"The sooner the better," his dad barked. "Then we can get out of this miserable, boring place, with these . . . sickeningly *nice* people."

Quentin knew his dad did not like Westbridge, Massachusetts. Little things made him grouchy— drivers yielding the right of way, people standing in lines politely, even when someone in the supermarket had eleven items instead of ten in the express line. Where his dad came from, *that* was grounds for a battle royale! And if there was anything Martin Pid liked, it was a good fight. Unfortunately, he'd found Westbridge way too complacent. He'd been reduced to blowing off steam at his own family at the movies—Quentin and his mom had to go along with it. But at least their silly antics had attracted Sabrina's attention. Which was the entire reason they were here in the first place.

"A day and a time, Quentin!" his dad was commanding impatiently. "Decide *now* when you're bringing her!"

Quentin hadn't figured that out exactly yet. But luck was with him once more tonight as the answer fell into his lap just a few minutes later. That's when the phone rang and Quentin ran into the kitchen to grab it. When he came back a minute later, he was aglow. "Is tomorrow night too soon? Sabrina just called—inviting us all to dinner at her house. What do you say?"

"Absolutely *not!*" Martin roared, slamming his fist down on the table, "She's to come to us! That's the way it works."

Veronica touched her husband's arm gently. "A lot of things have changed since we were here last, Martin. Let's do it their way. At the very least, we'll get a close-up view of our future . . . daughter-in-law."

"They're here! Omigosh, they're *here!*" Sabrina was a bundle of nerves. She'd changed her clothes so many times, her finger was actually tired. After all, what *is* the appropriate outfit for determining if your dinner guest is a warlock? Go find *that* advice in the latest *YM* magazine! And what about her hair? She'd switched styles countless times—from French twist, to ponytail, to half up, half down, clipped in the back. She settled on wearing it straight down with a zigzag part in the middle.

"Well, are you going to stand there and wring your hands, fretting, *'they're here, omigosh, they're here!'* or are you going to do something constructive and let them in?" Salem's imitation of Sabrina always made her sound like Minnie Mouse.

"Salem's right, Sabrina, answering the door

would be a good start," Zelda reminded her. She and Hilda had come in from the kitchen when the bell rang.

Sabrina took a deep breath and three steps toward the door. Little could have prepared her for the troika on the other side. As opposed to how they'd looked at the movies that night, this time it was as if they'd dressed for Halloween. Sabrina half expected them to thrust a shopping bag in her face and say, "Trick or treat." She was so stunned, she forgot her manners. Zelda and Hilda quickly ushered their guests in.

Up close, Quentin's mom, Veronica, was the most enchantingly beautiful woman Sabrina had ever seen. She shimmered in a pure white billowy confection of a dress. Her hair tumbled past her shoulders in golden waves, and her high-beam smile—much like Quentin's—was blinding. "Hi, I'm Veronica," she was saying as she extended a bejeweled hand toward Zelda. "It is so gracious of you to invite us into your home." Veronica offered Zelda a box of chocolates.

Hilda inserted herself into the introductions and accepted the chocolates. "Any friend of Sabrina's is a friend of ours. We've been anxious to meet the whole family." The sparkle in her eyes faded when she saw Quentin's dad.

For Martin looked like a caricature of an overage biker dude. A huge man, he wore a frayed black sleeveless T-shirt that revealed bulging, tattooed biceps. A profusion of gaudy gold chains hung around his neck. His thick black-streaked-with-gray hair was greased back; his beady black eyes seared into her. With an unintelligible grunt, he strode into the Spellman home as if he owned it.

"For you, Sabrina." Quentin, ensconced in his "lucky" brown leather bomber jacket, brought up the rear. He looked as amazingly gorgeous as ever, but seemed uncharacteristically nervous, practically thrusting a gift at Sabrina. "A boxed set of Violent Femmes CDs," he explained, "I heard you liked them."

You heard? From who? Only Harvey knew how much Sabrina was into that band. Going to an autograph signing had been one of her first sorta-dates with him. Sabrina pushed the memory to the back of her mind, pasted a thin smile on her face, and thanked Quentin. They followed the adults into the living room, where the awkward sextet commenced "getting to know you" small talk.

As soon as he sat down, Martin put his scuffed black biker boots up on the coffee table. Little bits of dirt embedded in the treads of his soles fell uncomfortably close to the hors d'oeuvres. Sabrina intuited, rather than saw, Zelda pointing up a doily underneath his feet, wiping the dirt, and moving the tray of canapes safely away from his boots. Martin seemed oblivious. He grabbed a handful of hors d'oeuvres, belched loudly, and demanded to know if Sabrina had prepared the food.

With a wink, aimed more at Veronica, Zelda answered, "Actually, we don't do a lot of cooking from scratch around here, if you know what I mean."

Veronica nodded enthusiastically. "I noticed! There are so many modern conveniences now. Prepared foods, frozen foods. I could see where you wouldn't even need servants."

Martin growled, "Where we come from, servants prepare our meals. From scratch." He shot a weird glance at Sabrina.

Hilda tilted her head and crooked her finger. "Well, we have our own little kitchen magicians always . . . *on hand.* If you know what I mean. . . ."

No one seemed to. Sabrina stole a glance at Quentin, who was staring uncomfortably at his Hush Puppied feet.

Sabrina felt as though she'd entered a strange new realm, so surrealistic was the scene in front of her. No matter what the topic, Veronica positively glowed, Martin gruffly scowled—breaking stride only when he gazed at his wife. Then, and only then, did he seem to soften. Meanwhile, Quentin seemed to shrink, more embarrassed with each passing moment.

The vibe didn't get any more comfortable when the group repaired to the dining room. Zelda and Hilda had concocted a full Greek-style dinner, from a feta-cheese dotted salad, and egg lemon soup, to souvlaki and lamb shish kebob served over rice. Veronica seemed strangely unfamiliar with anything on the menu and kept asking Hilda and Zelda for the recipes so she could pass them on to the servants. But when Hilda or Zelda intimated that they'd basically pointed everything up, Veronica seemed clueless. Finally Hilda took the bull by the horns, so to speak. She actually pointed to the lamb kabobs and magically added more rice. "See? Now you try it."

Veronica looked astonished. "Things *have* advanced since we were last here!" Then she shrugged her shoulders and aimed her forefinger at the exact spot Hilda had. Nothing appeared. Or disappeared.

Veronica giggled. "I guess I'm not quite assimilated yet."

Zelda stepped in, "You probably just need some practice."

Just then Veronica's eyes darted from Zelda to Hilda. She blurted out, "You two are such attractive, accomplished women. I bet you've had lots of suitors."

In other circumstances Sabrina and her aunts would have considered that comment totally rude, but playing along with the Pids might help them uncover who the bizarro bunch really were. So Zelda admitted that over the years—many, *many* years, she stressed—she'd enjoyed several serious and important relationships.

"But you haven't found your one, true love?" Veronica inquired, suddenly very interested. Before Zelda could answer, Veronica pointed at Quentin and Sabrina and said cryptically, "A love like theirs, you know, is very special. And not so impossible to find, if you know where to look. Or who to ask for help."

A love like theirs! Sabrina nearly choked. She blushed wildly, more angry than embarrassed. Even Quentin squirmed at his mother's outburst. It was left to Hilda, never at a loss for conversation, to save the awkward moment. She launched into an animated telling of her own roller coaster on-again, off-again, nonrelationship with Drell. Hilda was also trying to deduce if Veronica knew Drell. Any witch would, of course.

If Veronica did, she wasn't letting on. Instead, Quentin's mom seemed to take a deep interest in Hilda's love life. After dinner the two women actually went upstairs to look through Hilda's old photos of herself and Drell. As they climbed the stairs, Sabrina heard Veronica announce that this was a love that could be saved.

Sabrina shrugged and started to clear the dishes from the table. Quentin offered to help, but his loutish father grabbed his arm and forced him to sit down. "Men don't do dishes, you wuss," he blared. "Let her do them. She'd better get used to it anyway."

What? Sabrina was sure she must have misheard that last comment. No one could be as obnoxious as Quentin's dad—the whole thing had to be some sort of macho warlock act. All through dinner, when he wasn't stuffing himself or belching, he'd bragged about Quentin's victories in the archery tournaments. Martin made them sound more like wars between countries than high school athletic competitions.

Hilda and Veronica were still upstairs when Zelda called them down for coffee and dessert a while later. Keeping with the Greek theme, Sabrina's aunts had chosen to make baklava and pastries, which were now spread out on the table. Politely Zelda had also opened the box of chocolates the Pids brought. Witches loved chocolates: unlike that Forrest Gump "you never know what you're gonna get," comment, they could see past the coating. They always knew what they were gonna get.

Salem had spent much of the evening perched on the mantel, but the selection of tasties on the table was too much temptation. He hopped up next to Sabrina, hungrily eyeing the baklava. Sabrina stroked Salem's back and broke off a crusty piece for him.

Martin seemed grossed out by the gesture. "Isn't that cute," he drawled sarcastically, "Sabby and her tabby."

Sabrina bristled. Was the whole family nickname-obsessed? Her stunned silence allowed Martin to continue, disapprovingly, "Where we come from, lower life-forms are barred from the dinner table."

Lower life-forms! Talk about the pot calling the kettle black! Salem couldn't decide which disparaging appellation he was more steamed about. He arched his back, leaped in front of Martin, and hissed, "Tabby! I'm a purebred American short-hair, buster. Unlike you, the mutt of warlocks."

Amazingly, Martin didn't take the bait. He merely yawned and grabbed a handful of baklavas. Which meant two things: Salem wasn't worth fighting, and he wasn't fazed by a talking cat. If Martin was a warlock, he would have instantly recognized one of his own kind in Salem.

The Pids departed shortly after dessert, but not without issuing a return invite—to Sabrina. "You *must* come see us," Veronica insisted. "Quentin will bring you."

"Well, this ranks right up there with my Top Ten weirdest evenings," Sabrina declared, closing the door after them and returning to the kitchen to finish cleaning up.

Zelda seemed especially perplexed. "If they're witches like us, they're doing an admirable job of obfuscating any evidence."

"That, and two paws up for how well they're hiding it," Salem added as he jumped onto the table for leftover desserts.

"Obfuscate means to purposely confuse things," Sabrina informed the cat. "Didn't they teach vo-cabulary back in the Middle Ages?"

Zelda shook her head. She'd made up her mind. "I hate to disappoint you, Sabrina, but based on the evidence of this evening, the Pids have to be mortal. They are strange, that's for sure. Martin's probably the most obnoxious male I've ever encountered, and that includes several centuries' worth of jerks. And Veronica's beautiful, but an airhead. Quentin seems the most normal of them all, I'm afraid."

Salem stopped licking the pastries long enough to agree. "I'm casting my vote for disgusting, weird, gross, bubble-head—and mortal."

Sabrina turned to the portrait of Aunt Louisa on the kitchen wall. The portrait had her own unique angle on the comings and goings of the Spellman household. But she, too, came down in favor of the "not a warlock" theory.

Only Aunt Hilda remained strangely silent. In fact, Sabrina's normally bubbly, talkative aunt had been unusually quiet ever since she and Veronica had come downstairs for dessert. She hadn't even seen the Pids to the door, but remained at the kitchen table, seemingly lost in space.

"What do you think, Aunt Hilda?" Sabrina finally asked. The sound of Sabrina's voice seemed to rouse her from her reverie. She focused on her niece, and her own voice was clear and deliberate, most un-Hilda-like. "No, they're not."

"Uh, could you vague that up for me? No, they're not . . . what?"

"Mortal. They're not mortal."

Zelda, Sabrina, and Salem snapped to attention.

"Give it up," Salem commanded. "What do you know and when did you know it?"

Hilda took a deep breath. And another. A third. Finally, she spilled. "From the minute that Veronica walked in the door, I knew there was something familiar about her. I just couldn't place it. So when we went upstairs to look through some photos, I asked her what her maiden name was. She said De Milo. And then I said, 'This is so six degrees of separation-y. I went to school with a girl whose last name was De Milo, but I don't think her first name was Veronica.' When she turned her back, I dug out my elementary school yearbook and flipped to the *D*'s—well, what do you know? It turns out that V. De Milo—we didn't put first names down in yearbooks in those days—was in my second-grade class! It was her!"

"That is *so* amazing!" Sabrina couldn't believe the coincidence.

Then Hilda zapped her back to reality.

"Second grade was six hundred years ago, Sabrina. For both of us."

Chapter 8

☆

Sabrina and Zelda were stunned into silence. Salem broke it. "Okay, ladies, let's recap, shall we? We've established that Mama Pid, anyway, is not mortal. Him I still have my doubts about. The kid's up in the air as far as I'm concerned. So who are they? And *why* are they?"

Sabrina felt hopeful. "They're probably long-lost relatives, that's it. Ergo, Quentin and I could never be boyfriend and girlfriend. Only . . . he doesn't know it yet. . . ." She trailed off, realizing the tangent she was on was about to dead end.

"Maybe Quentin's really a cat, forced to do penance in the body of a Greek godlike teenager," Salem snickered, leaping out of the way quickly to avoid a swipe from Sabrina.

Zelda went over to the rolltop desk and extracted her laptop computer. "There must be a scientific answer to this." She started keyboarding, scrolling, clicking and pointing, cutting and pasting, but all that came up on the screen was "bad file command" and "not enough memory to continue operation." Surfing the Internet came up with no helpful websites. And not even Zelda's advanced witch capabilities could get her past the busy signals of America Online. Frustrated, she slammed the computer shut.

"Let's just do it the old-fashioned way," Hilda suggested. "Let's carefully inspect the family tree. Maybe there's a distant branch we didn't know about."

Zelda shrugged. "I can't come up with a better idea."

Sabrina didn't know a family tree existed. She trailed her aunts and Salem as they headed out the back door. "We keep our family tree . . . in the backyard?" she asked incredulously.

"You got a better place for this abomination?" Salem responded as he headed toward the far end of the yard. Sabrina's eyes followed his path. He stopped in front of a huge hardwood tree. Because it was winter, the tree was bare of leaves, but it did have an intricate variety of branches, not all of them up top, either. Random twigs stuck out from all angles, all up and down the trunk.

"This is our family tree?" Sabrina asked, wide-eyed, as the trio drew nearer to the lofty, hulking hardwood. "How come I've never noticed it before?"

"Maybe you've never really looked before," Zelda said as she began circling it, and pointing. With each flick of her finger, a new leaf magically appeared. Sabrina walked up and examined the first one. It had a name on it: "Edward Spellman."

"That's my dad!" she said jubilantly. "Make my leaf appear!"

Zelda did, explaining, "I've started with our immediate family, and we'll go outward from there. Eventually, we should uncover almost every known witch in all realms. Hilda, you start on the other side of the tree, with cousin Monty's clan."

Hilda pouted. "Why do I get stuck with them?"

At Zelda's no-nonsense glance she capitulated. "Oh, all right. But we're doing this for Sabrina. And . . . because I never liked Veronica, she was gorgeous even in second grade. And she made me feel like . . . such a lumpy witch. If I could only remember what name she went by then. . . ."

Ignoring her sister, Zelda instructed, "Sabrina, levitate a few feet in the air and start with cousin Tanya's branch of the family. Just point and click."

Sabrina happily levitated and began the leaf-search. Salem was enlisted to help, but he couldn't resist using the tree as a scratching post. He came up empty-pawed.

Unfortunately, so did the three witches. After a laborious hour of turning over every leaf on every branch of the family tree, they found no Pids.

"Well, they're not part of our happy little witch family, that's for sure," Hilda concluded wearily.

"Well, Quentin's still never going to be my boyfriend, *that's* for sure," Sabrina added forcefully as she floated down from the higher branches, hitting the ground a little harder than intended.

"There *is* one other scenario," Zelda ventured. "If they're in the Witchness Protection Program, they would have been plucked off this tree. That would account for their cover-up behavior, too."

"But not for their weirdness," Salem said. "I hate to say it, but there's only one person who'll know the truth. Our fearless, if misguided, leader."

Hilda groaned. "No, I'm not going to see Drell. Just talking about him with Veronica opened up painful wounds. Count me out."

Hilda didn't really mean that. For neither witch nor mortal seemed able to avoid that "Smart Women, Foolish Choices" trap. Hilda couldn't resist a visit with her former—and no doubt in her mind, future—flame. Besides, the cat was right. If the Pids had even a trace of witch blood in them, Drell would know.

Sabrina and Zelda marched into the house and up the stairs toward the linen closet. Hilda was right behind, rationalizing all the way. "I'm doing this just so Sabrina can get some answers. We're all clear on that, right?"

The linen closet was a shortcut to the Other Realm. Of course, it was also a linen closet. To the mortal eye, only sheets, towels, and several half-opened containers of fabric softener were visible. But once the door closed and lightning struck, witches were instantly transported through the Bed and Bath section to the Beyond. That's where Drell, the head of the Witches' Council, sat in judgment every day from nine to three Monday to Friday. "Bankers' hours," he'd decreed. "For all other appointments, have your people call my people."

Hilda, of course, knew exactly how to summon Drell any time of the day or night. And once Sabrina and her aunts arrived in Drell's lair, she did. She picked up a bullhorn and called out gaily, "I'm here for our date," pretending Drell had forgotten to wiggle out of one.

It did the trick. Instantly he appeared. Drell was a big man. Huge, really. His shoulder-length, frizzy unkempt hair meant to give him a wild, scary appearance. Instead, all it did was make you want to tame those split ends with an economy-size bottle of shampoo. Drell seemed nervous and eyed Hilda suspiciously. "We had . . . a date?" he gulped, "I don't seem to have it on my agenda."

Hilda put down the bullhorn and looked him in the eye. "What you mean is, you can't find the notation to break it."

Drell laughed self-consciously. "Hilda, Hilda, Hilda. My dear Hilda. What can I say? I'm overwhelmed here. Being the head of the Witches' Council is very demanding. And since they downsized my department, I don't even have a junior executive assistant anymore. I've had to sacrifice my personal life . . ."

Hilda held her hand up. "Relax, Drell. I didn't come about a date."

Relieved, Drell said, "You didn't? You mean, that was just a ploy to get me into my office on a Saturday night? Hilda, you're a cagey one."

Zelda jumped in. "We're here because we've got a thorny little problem and we need your help." She motioned to Sabrina. "Tell him."

As Drell stroked his chin, and tried to appear regal, Sabrina described the Pids and all the weird events of the past several weeks—ending with the part about Veronica and Hilda being in second grade together. "We need to know if you know them. We think they might be in the Witchness Protection Program and that's why they obfuscated evidence."

"Obfuscated?" Drell seemed impressed. "An SAT word, Sabrina! Excellent! You know we have special prep courses for that. . . ."

"Can we focus, Drell?" Zelda brought him back. "Just look them up for us. It's very important to Sabrina, and by now, we're all beyond curious."

Drell winked at Hilda. "Off the top of my head, I have no personal knowledge of them. Which means that if they are witches, they're hardly worth knowing. But if it's important to *you*—my dear Hilda— I'll sacrifice my off-duty time to find out."

Drell strolled over to his giant mahogany desk and, with great feigned effort, extracted a thick, oversize phone book. "Let's just see now. How'd you say the name was spelled?" He turned to the *P*'s.

"Hmmm. Pilates? No, that's a new aerobics course. Portnoy? No, he just complains a lot. Here we go . . . no, that's not them. Let's . . ." Drell made all sorts of grunts and noises, but Hilda could tell all he was really doing was running his finger down the list of names that began with *P*.

"Sometime *this* century, Drell," Sabrina's aunt urged. "Unlike *next* century, when we might actually *go* on a date."

Abruptly Drell slammed the phone book closed. "They're not here. I checked the Witchness Protection Program, and they're not listed there, either. No M. Pid, no V. Pid, no Q. Pid. Ergo, they don't exist. Sorry, ladies."

Sabrina felt the air go out of her. Zelda and Hilda sighed in tandem.

Drell walked over and put a consoling arm around Hilda. "Sorry I couldn't help you gals. But as long as you're here . . . Hilda . . . would you like to join me in the inner lair? It's so lonely at the top, you know. The pleasure of your unannounced company is sweetly appealing. Stay awhile."

Hilda smiled coquettishly. Sabrina couldn't believe it—Hilda was actually falling for his tired old lines all over again? She was about to grab her aunt's sleeve and pull her away, but Zelda interceded. "She's a grown woman, Sabrina. She can make her own decisions. Just like you'll have to."

Just like I'll have to, Sabrina thought morosely as she and Zelda spirited themselves back through the linen closet. *Drell may be dreck, but at least Hilda knows* what *he is.*

I'm still clueless about Quentin.

Veronica Pid was flabbergasted. As soon as they'd returned home from dinner at the Spellmans, she began pacing and shaking her golden curls. *"She's* the most ravishing ingenue this generation could come up with? What a hoot! Her hair is at least seven inches too short and she can't even comb a straight part into it! And deal, for a minute, with that outfit she had on! Pul-eeeze, darlings! Why, she's hardly worth bothering with! She can't be the one, my son."

Quentin held firm. "She's *got* to be the one, Mom. I know she doesn't look exactly like we imagined, but it's 1998. Perceptions of beauty are different now. I think she's cute. Bewitching, even."

Martin broke in, "She's no Aphrodite. Sheesh, she's not even Xena. But I see what the kid sees in Sabrina. She's fiery. Spunky. It's all buried beneath the surface, waiting to explode. But what's she doing living with those biddy aunts? And that cat! I'd like to strangle it. When she comes with us, she won't be leaving much behind."

Veronica sighed and flopped onto the couch. "If you're sure, Quentin, let's get this charade over with. Though I admit a fascination with that hapless Hilda—there's something familiar about her, though I can't place it. Her choice in men is abominable! That drecky Drell, she showed me his picture—ugh! Talk about having a bad hair life . . ."

Veronica yawned and called out to her son. "Maybe as a lovely parting gift, you can help that Hilda out. . . ." Then, she fell asleep, still fully dressed.

Sabrina spent the rest of the weekend trying to figure Quentin out. The better she got to know him, the more confused she became. Okay, his mother wasn't mortal, but she wasn't a witch, either. Not that Drell would divulge, anyway. His father was just . . . ugh, too gross to contemplate. Quentin himself was . . . what? Resistant to her magic and determined to be her boyfriend. After all this time, that was the sum total of what she knew. The who, what, where, how, and especially *why* remained elusive. Not to mention when, or how she and Harvey would ever get back on track. From what she'd seen and heard, Harvey and Jenny remained "closerthanthis."

Still, she refused to totally give up hope. Sabrina routinely left cutesy messages on his answering machine—Harvey was never home!—even though she knew he probably wouldn't return them. Same with Jenny. Sabrina tried to pretend nothing had changed between the two friends. And Jenny was friendly enough. Never available to hang with Sabrina, though.

By Monday morning—the last week before Valentine's Day Saturday, she noted glumly—Sabrina felt she'd run out of options. Somehow, *even if she had to reveal her own secret to expose his,* Sabrina would unearth the truth.

Monday was the day of the semifinal archery match in the state championship. It was Westbridge versus another leading team, Southvale High. Southvale had worked hard to move up through the ranks. Probably because they had a lot riding on a win. It just so happened that school was in an underprivileged district badly in need of that new athletic facility that business consortium had pledged. But a Southvale win didn't seem likely. The Westbridge Archers, riding an unbroken winning streak, were a lock to go all the way. Just in case, however, Principal Conroy had excused the team from afternoon classes so they could practice. They were out on the field all afternoon.

That's when Sabrina impulsively decided to raid Quentin's locker—he *could* be hiding a secret there, she reasoned. Gaining access to the boys' locker room was a snap. *Maybe I can't use my magic on him, but I can still use it on me.* She made herself invisible.

A quick check of the locker room assured her that it was deserted, but she elected to stay invisible just in case. She scouted all around for the locker with Quentin's name taped on it. At first she couldn't find it. She did find Harvey's, though, and on a whim scribbled a "Good Luck" message on a tissue and slipped it inside.

Finally, in a distant corner, she saw the one marked Quentin Pid. *Strange that it's so far from any of the others,* she noted. *You'd think he'd want to be close to his team. Oh, well—*

Was his locker immune to her, too?

She never got the chance to find out.

Her finger was poised in the air, but just at the second of magical release, she heard the main locker room door bang open. She had company. He was singing a familiar song. "All You Need Is Love."

Quentin.

Sabrina was invisible to the *mortal* eye—but could *Quentin* see her? Silently she backed away from his locker. The footsteps got closer and his singing, louder. His repetition of the same verse was grating. "Love, love, love . . . love is all you need, love is all you need, love is all you need, *every*body! . . ." Good thing he didn't go out for chorus, Sabrina thought, holding her breath.

Quentin headed straight for the back of the locker room. He stopped directly in front of his locker and abruptly ceased singing. He listened carefully, then peered around to be absolutely certain he was alone. Sabrina, who was right behind him, dared not breathe.

Secure in his solitude, Quentin relaxed and began to hum, twirling his combination lock open.

Now! I'll make myself visible and confront him now!

Sabrina was just about to point at herself, when Quentin flung open his locker and quickly removed that ever-present bomber jacket. Mesmerized, Sabrina watched as he tossed it on the bench. Then he unbuttoned his long-sleeved white shirt. Suddenly embarrassed, she half-turned away when he took it off.

That's when she saw his back. She'd never seen anything quite like it, on a mortal, or a fellow witch. Permanently attached, just below his shoulder blades, was a pair of golden wings.

Chapter 9

☆

☆

Stunned, Sabrina gasped in astonishment. Quentin spun around. Panicked, he cried, "Who's there?" He grabbed his shirt and hastily threw it over his shoulders, covering his back. "Who's there?" he called out again, louder. He was obviously alarmed. His eyes darted up and down the row of lockers as he clumsily tried to rebutton his shirt.

Sabrina was hyperventilating. But as she pointed herself visible, all at once, everything crystalized. The voice she heard in her head was Drell's. His words rang out as loudly as if he were standing right there, bellowing in her ear. *"No V. Pid, no Z. Pid . . ."*

". . . no Q. Pid."

Curly golden-blond ringlets. Archery champion. Love spells! And now an incontrovertible truth: a set of golden wings. Which the ever-present leather bomber jacket efficiently hid.

There was only one question that remained in Sabrina's mind: *If you looked up* dense *in the dictionary, would my picture be there?*

Fully materialized, and still breathing hard, Sabrina stared at him in total amazement. He stared back. Finally she caught her breath long enough to stammer, "Cupid. You're . . . you're . . . Cupid."

Quentin took a step toward her. The panic was gone from his eyes. He should have been dumbfounded, stunned, amazed at the very least, at Sabrina's ability to emerge before him. He also should have been terrified that she obviously now knew his secret.

Strangely, Quentin felt none of those emotions. Instead, a mixture of love and relief washed over him. He let out a long sigh and cupped Sabrina's face in his hands. "It took you long enough to figure it out, my beautiful Psyche."

That name again! Only he kept pronouncing it "sy-kee," instead of just plain "sike," as in "I faked you out." Sabrina took a step back and shook her head. "You can't psyche me out. I *know.* I saw your . . . your . . . uh . . ." She could barely bring herself to say it. "I saw those . . . wingie thingies."

Quentin chuckled and covered her hands with his. "I'm not trying to psyche you out, Sabrina. I'm telling you that I know who *you* really are."

"You do?"

"Of course I know," Quentin insisted. "You're the reason I came to New England. In this century, that is. My family and I have been looking for you."

"You have?" Now Sabrina was getting seriously nervous. She slipped her hands out from his.

Quentin tapped the bench and sat down. "Sit down, my beloved."

Sabrina didn't move.

Quentin coaxed, "Come on, I'll explain everything. I know you're dying to know—that *is* why you sneaked into the boys' locker room, isn't it?"

He was right, but Sabrina was conflicted. The truth was in here—only she wasn't sure she was ready for it. Gently Quentin took her hand again. Hesitantly she eased onto the bench next to him.

"Okay, Quen . . . uh, Cupid, that is. You really are Cupid, aren't you? I mean, the wings, the bow and arrow, the whole, uh, package. . . ." She felt incredibly bizarre saying it.

He felt incredibly relieved that she did. His eyes twinkled. "I really am. In the flesh, as it were. And I'm here because of you. We came to find you. You and I are destined to be together forever. . . ."

Freaked, Sabrina popped up. "Noooo, that's where you're mistaken, Cupey, boy. We are so not destined. Not in any way, shape, or—"

Quentin reached out and gently coaxed her back down. "Just listen, okay? I live on Mount Olympus. Don't bother dragging out the atlas, it's in another dimension. Anyway, we've lived there, pretty much for centuries. But every once in a while we're summoned to Earth—"

"We?" Sabrina interrupted. "Who else is here with you?"

"My parents, of course. You've met them. My mom, Veronica. Well, her real name is Venus. She's the Goddess of Love. My dad—at home he's known as Mars—is the God of War—"

"That explains a lot!" Sabrina exclaimed. No wonder Veronica—née Venus—was so other-worldly beautiful. And Martin . . . Mars, that is, so quarrelsome. It all made sense—albeit in a very strange, no one will *ever* believe this, kind of way. Sort of like being a witch in 1998.

But none of it explained *why* they had infused themselves into *her* life. Sabrina prompted, "What are you doing here? Isn't Cupid's job to patch some love crisis or something? I mean, here in West-bridge, everything was fine—until you came along and messed it up."

He protested, "I didn't mess it up. I un-messed it up. See, you're supposed to belong to me, not to some Harvey jerk. I came to get you."

Sabrina was aghast. "I'm *supposed* to *belong* to you? That's ridiculous! Where'd you get that from?"

Defiantly Quentin retorted, "Legend. That's where! I'm Cupid. You're Psyche. I find you, we fall in love, you come with me, we live happily ever—"

"No way!" Sabrina shrieked, jumping up again.

"Yes, way!" Quentin contradicted, steamed. "Look, Psyche, I don't make up the legends, I only obey them. As you must."

Sabrina was flabbergasted. This . . . person . . . boy . . . Greek God, actually, in front of her was *serious*. This wasn't some bizarre joke Libby or jealous cousin Tanya had concocted, and it wasn't even a test her aunts had devised. This would be news even to them!

"Besides," Quentin continued with a conspiratorial wink, "many gifts await when you come with me. . . ."

Sabrina held her hand up. "Save it. It was all very sweet, the boxed CD set, the flowers and the candy, but I don't want any gifts from you."

"Oh, I think you'll want this one," he said, lowering his voice, although no one else was in the locker room. "I can give you the gift of immortality."

Sabrina sighed. "Been there. Done that. Bought the T-shirt."

Quentin was starting to chafe. "Psyche, I'm serious."

"So am I. And stop calling me that. It's worse than Sab. And what could possibly make you think *I* was this Psyche babe anyway?"

Quentin shrugged. "Simple. My mom told me Psyche was here on Earth, in this century, and it was our destiny to find her and bring her back. And after scoping all the girls on earth, it was obvious: You were the most magical."

So I was wrong. He didn't know I was a witch; he thought I was some mythical chick.

Sabrina sucked in her breath. "Magical, huh? Uh, Quen . . . Cupid . . . there's kind of a reason for that. It's also the reason I don't need your gift of immortality."

And then, for the first time since finding out she was a witch, Sabrina actually told someone outside her family. All of it, including her own predestination for immortality.

Sabrina had always fantasized that one day she'd tell Harvey. One day, years from now, when they were really serious, and about to get married. Well, Quentin, Cupid, whoever he was, wasn't Harvey. He wasn't even technically a friend, and no matter what he or his family envisioned, that happily-ever-after thing was so not happening. But she couldn't help how she felt. Which was . . . kinda . . . good.

It was liberating to share her secret with someone who at least looked her age, even though she knew he wasn't. Cupid had been around for centuries and could take on the body of anyone he wanted. This time, as any girl would agree, he'd chosen *really* well.

Sabrina gazed into Cupid's clear blue eyes, admitting, "I kept trying to use my magic on you, but it never worked. Now I know why."

But if Sabrina thought that by telling him the

truth, he'd wake up and smell the fungi, she was in for another big shock. Quentin didn't believe her!

His gaze met hers. "I know what you're doing, Psyche. I read the advice magazines. I read that book, *The Rules*. You're playing hard-to-get. But you can't fool Mother Legend. None of your twentieth century psychobabble applies. My arrows pierced your heart and you are in love with me, just as destiny has willed it."

Sabrina couldn't believe what she was hearing. She'd just told him her deepest secret, and he barely heard her! He refused to get off that destiny kick.

Determined, she folded her arms across her chest. "I'm not playing games. I don't love you, Quentin."

"Okay, okay, I'll admit my first arrow didn't take. Maybe I was a little rusty in the clutch. But the one I shot at you at close range, in the car on our date, *that one did the trick*. I shot, you kissed me instantly, did you not?"

Sabrina rubbed her temples. "Quentin, you are deluded. You *pretended* to shoot. Did you think I'd sit there and let you hit me with an actual arrow?"

Quentin seemed to look right through her. "My love arrows are invisible, Sabrina. Didn't you know that?"

Uh, actually, no. She didn't. Apparently, there was a lot of Greek mythology she didn't know. But she had to set Quentin straight. Now. "Quentin, maybe you did, as you say, shoot me with some weird invisible love arrow. You probably even shot the whole school with them! But were you listening to me? I'm a witch—I'm immune to your spells. I kissed you because I thought you were mortal. And a witch's kiss—to a boy she doesn't love—turns a mortal into a frog. It was my plan to get rid of you."

Quentin grinned, victorious. "That proves it, Pysche—you just said it yourself. If you didn't love me, I would have turned into a frog. I didn't—ergo, you do. Love me that is."

"Ergo! All it proves is that you're not mortal. And if that weren't proof enough, you've got that wing thing happening. . . ."

Quentin laughed. "You know what, Sab . . . this doesn't change anything. Say what you will to me, I know the truth. You are Psyche, you are in love with me. And after the archery tournament you're coming home with me."

Sabrina closed her eyes, exasperated. In a contest for who's denser, he had her beat by a realm or two. Abruptly Quentin got up. "Gotta get ready, Psyche—the rest of the team will be here any minute to change for the tournament. You're going to come watch us clobber Southvale, aren't you?"

Sabrina's eyes flew open as another truth dawned on her. "Tell me something, Cupid. What's with the tournament? How did our team suddenly become archery champs? You had something to do with it, didn't you?"

His back to her, he opened his locker to change

his shirt—giving Sabrina another chance to gape at his wings. They were actually . . . kind of awesome. They folded in toward each other, which sort of flattened them, but not completely. And they glittered.

He snorted, "The Westbridge Archers—what a joke! They stink at archery. Even I'm not *that* good. But I am excellent at cheating. I used my own magic to ensure that their pathetic little efforts actually hit the target. I concentrated and *willed* it to happen. I can do that, you know!"

Sabrina was perplexed. "But *why* would you do that?"

Quentin shrugged. "In the current vernacular, I believe the explanation would be, 'Well, *duh.*'"

"What's *duh* got to do with it? Cupid is supposed to be about love. This has nothing to do with love. You're cheating the other schools' more deserving teams out of a win. What's the point?"

Quentin was irked. "What's *your* point? Of course I cheat. It's my nature to cheat."

It is? Apparently, she had a lot to learn about Cupid. The real Cupid.

But later for that. Sabrina couldn't sit idly by, knowing that Quentin had cheated all through the archery tournament and was about to do it again. And this time, to a team more deserving, and in real need of the win. In a flash she made up her mind to change *his* mind.

"Quen . . . I mean Cupe. Okay, so maybe it's your nature to cheat. But it's not mine. As your, uh, destiny babe . . ." Sabrina felt herself gagging, but continued, "Is there anything I can do to make you play *this* match fair and square?"

"Well," he mused, slowly turning around to her and stroking his chin. "I am susceptible to bribes. You can bribe me."

"Bribe you! I don't believe you. . . ." Sabrina was aghast. But then she thought about Harvey, and about Southvale. If she acquiesced to Quentin's suggestion, it might be one small step toward setting things right. Which could lead to other steps. She took a deep breath.

"If I bribe you with a kiss—would you agree not to cheat at this match?"

Quentin regarded her. Then he broke out in one of his megawatt smiles and pointed at his lips. "Plant one. Right here."

Once again, Sabrina crossed her fingers behind her back: She kept the bribe kiss short and sweet.

Luckily, it was enough to do the trick. For an hour later, when Quentin and the Westbridge Archers took the field to face the Southvale Quivers, something happened that hadn't occurred since BQ: Before Quentin. Westbridge seemed to . . . implode.

As each archer took his or her position, secured the arrow, and aimed, the crowd held its breath in anticipation of a bull's-eye. Instead, one by one, the arrows released totally tanked.

Raymond Jackson's arrow had some velocity to

it—only it went in the wrong direction, veering crazily toward the stands. Everyone ducked out of the way! Raymond was flabbergasted and asked for a do-over. It was denied. His Southvale competitor didn't hit a bull's-eye, but hit the target, racking up points.

Rebecca Larson's arrow had some power behind it, too. Only hers flew straight up in the air and came down with a thud, just inches from her feet. The crowd let out a collective gasp. There were tears in Rebecca's eyes as she turned and walked away. Her Southvale partner didn't waste time. She managed to rack up fifty points with a competent shot.

The Westbridge crowd had gotten very quiet. Even the cheerleaders, led by the usually indomitable Libby, retreated, trying to save face.

Then came Harvey. For a second Sabrina herself was tempted to help him out and crooked her finger. But she remembered the big picture. Normally, Harvey stank at archery. If he was ever going to get back to normal, and to her, he'd have to fail on his own.

He did, spectacularly. His arrow left the bow with a whimper and fell miserably to the ground a few feet from where Harvey stood. He was dumbfounded. He loped over, picked his arrow up, studied it for imperfections, and, crestfallen, trudged off the field.

No one could understand what was happening. No one but Sabrina and Quentin, that is. The

Southvale team began to feel the real possibility of a victory. Indeed, they were cruising to a crusher. Their cheerleaders came alive.

Quentin was up last for Westbridge. By that time there was no way one person could affect the outcome. The best he could do was save Westbridge from being completely taco-ed. Only Quentin had no motivation. He'd never cared about winning at archery; winning Sabrina was his goal. He had that, firmly in hand. Instead of even bothering to aim for the target, Quentin withdrew a fistful of arrows from his quiver and began shooting them wildly in the air.

He was sincerely startled when everyone started booing him! *Hey, hold on a minute, there, mortals! For the past three weeks I've been your hero! You would have elected me President if you could have! And now, just because of a stupid archery tournament, you've turned on me? What's that about?*

In fact, Quentin hadn't expected to feel badly about the loss—but he hadn't expected the jeers of his newfound peers, either. They pierced his confidence. He actually felt pretty crummy.

Chapter 10

Quentin didn't bother returning to the lockers. He looked for Sabrina, but she was nowhere to be found. Whatever. *She loves me, she's not going far,* he thought as he climbed into his car and headed home. Quentin wasn't normally susceptible to introspection, and he wasn't very good at it. He never understood what was so important about the tournament to these mortals.

Quentin's goal in coming to Earth, in coming to Westbridge specifically, was to follow his mother's instructions and nab Psyche. It had taken him longer than expected, but he had to admit, he was kind of grooving on it now that he was here. The food was great—that whole food court concept? Brilliant! He liked the malls, video games, and stuff like MTV. Even that rock band Sabrina was into wasn't bad. It was fun being a teenager in 1998.

And such a popular one! Everyone adored him. More girls would have had crushed on him if he hadn't shot them with love arrows and made them fall for other boys. He couldn't understand how his popularity had fallen apart just like that. How he could be knocked off his pedestal so quickly. Geez!

He was still feeling uncharacteristically dejected when he got home. Usually Quentin announced his presence in song. But this time he entered the house quietly. Which is probably why his parents didn't hear him come in.

But he heard them. Venus and Mars were arguing. He was about to make his presence known, when he realized they were talking about *him*. Quentin snuck behind the drapes in the living room and listened.

His father was snarling, "So, my darling, in your twisted little way, you managed to get what you wanted—but only because your son is so gullible. Took you long enough, though, didn't it?"

Veronica snapped, "Why is it twisted? Just because I go about winning my battles without bloodshed, unlike you! I've been trying to teach you for centuries, Mars, you trap more bees with honey than with . . ."

"Bees! We didn't come for bees! We came to grab Psyche and allay your jealous fears, Venus." Then Mars's voice softened, "I do love your jealous nature, honey, especially when it leads you to nefarious schemes, like this one did."

Quentin couldn't believe his ears. His going after Psyche had something to do with his mother's . . . jealousy? That made no sense at all. She never told him that! But as Quentin continued to listen, it became clearer.

"I don't see it as nefarious, Mars. But when I found out, through the grapevine back on Mount Olympus, of the existence of a young girl, more beautiful than I! Well, how would you expect me to feel? I am Venus, the Goddess of Love. There *can't* be anyone more glorious than I, in any century, in any universe, in any dimension. Imagine how mythology books would be affected! I had to manipulate a little readjustment."

Martin grunted, "Ah, but you deviated from your original plan, did you not, my darling? And thereby, invoked the help of your naive son."

Veronica bristled. "Well, the original legend is dated. It said Cupid was supposed to come to Earth and make Psyche fall in love with a *dragon*. Well, hello, we've been here a month—have you seen any suitable dragons? So, naturally, I had to go to Plan B. Luckily, I had access to the Internet down here. And I learned that updated legends have Cupid himself falling in love with Psyche, luring her into our lair, marrying her even. Which is more romantic!"

Quentin could hear his father rub his hands with glee. "Romantic my foot! Once she's settled on Mount Olympus, you'll turn your darling daughter-in-law into a slave. She'll be reduced to menial labor. She'll have to throw out the garbage, walk the dog, empty the kitty litter, make the beds, cook festive meals for us. Then Cupid's beloved Psyche, weighted down with drudgery, will age quickly and no longer be a threat to your beauty. Ensuring that you, my darling Venus, will remain the one and only unstoppable Love Goddess. Is that about right?"

Veronica murmured, "Well, maybe. Something like that. But you make it sound so calculated, when it's merely self-defense. Holding one's own footing in today's convoluted universes is so difficult. Besides, Cupid will get over her."

Mars snickered. "Enlisting Cupid's unknowing help was a brilliant strategic maneuver. Your son is so gullible! It's a good thing he was born with those wings. He'd never cut it as a warrior."

"My son! He's your son, too, Mars. But I for one am glad he's a lover, not a fighter. One War God in the family is quite enough, thank you!"

Quentin's jaw hung open as his parents revealed the depth of their deception. A tear began to fall.

Silently Quentin slipped out from behind the curtains. He was too distraught to confront his parents. Instead, he dashed out of the house, jumped behind the wheel of his car, and drove aimlessly through the streets. It wasn't until he turned onto Collins Road that he realized where he was: at Sabrina's.

Hilda responded to the doorbell. If Sabrina's

aunt was surprised to see Quentin, she didn't show it. Nor did she exhibit outward shock when he said, "I'm here to see Psyche. Is she here?"

"There's no one here by that name, Quentin, but if you meant Sabrina, she's upstairs. Wait here, I'll call her."

Hilda didn't have to. Sabrina had been at the top of the steps and heard everything. What struck her wasn't so much Quentin asking to see Psyche, but the tone of his voice. Really morose.

Sabrina assumed he was bummed over the way he'd been jeered after the tournament. She felt obligated to cheer him up, since it was her idea that he cheat . . . that is, not cheat and lose honestly.

"Hey, Cu . . . Quentin," she burbled, bouncing down the steps, "Come on in." Then Sabrina turned to Hilda. "Would it be okay if, uh, Quentin and I could talk, privately? Would you mind going to the—"

Sabrina didn't have to finish her sentence. "I was just getting hungry," Hilda said with a dismissive wave. "I'll go help Zelda with dinner. Come on Salem."

Sabrina motioned for Quentin to follow her into the living room. "Look, I know it must have felt strange to you, but by not cheating, you did a good thing. Southvale made it to the state championship and could win a badly needed athletic field. And it's all thanks to . . . this is *so weird!* . . . to the fact that you didn't cheat. I know the kids booed you and you probably feel cruddy about that . . ."

Quentin held his hand up, stopping her. "Past tense. I did feel bad about that. But when I got home, I got a lesson in the real meaning of cruddy."

"Your parents were upset that you played by the rules?" she guessed.

"Huh! Not quite. I found out that they . . . they *lied* to me, Psyche! They've been lying to me all this time! They used me! They . . ." Quentin could barely continue. He began to pace and wring his hands. Finally he blurted out the whole story, ending with a passionate cry, "They're going to make you a slave! I can't let that happen. Because . . . I really love you."

Sabrina let out an exasperated sigh. The phrase "one step forward and two steps back" came to her. Maybe she *had* gotten Quentin to play fair at the archery tournament, but she'd made less than zero progress on the "I'm not Psyche and we don't love each other" front. Apparently, after overhearing his parents lay bare their scheme, he was more convinced than ever that she was Psyche—and he was in love with her. And, uh, vice versa.

Sabrina knew she needed reinforcements. She called them.

"Aunt Zelda, Aunt Hilda . . . Salem . . . I'd like you to meet"—Sabrina sucked her breath in—"Cupid."

Zelda's hand flew to her mouth. For Sabrina's brainy aunt instantly understood. "Quentin Pid. Q. Pid," she murmured in recognition. "No wonder we couldn't figure it out. We were barking up the wrong tree. As it were."

"Scratching up the wrong tree," Salem said, still suspicious. "We never did bother with the whole mythological universe tree in the front yard."

Hilda was still flummoxed. "Cupid? But Cupid's not real. He's a . . ."

". . . a figure in Greek mythology," Zelda explained. "Who comes to Earth every so often whenever he's needed to deliver the gift of love to hearts that are too pure to be lonely. Isn't that right?"

Quentin nodded. "Except that wasn't the mission this time." Together, Quentin and Sabrina told Hilda, Zelda, and Salem the whole story. The Pids had been scoping Sabrina for a long time. Making a spectacle of themselves at the movies was all planned. As was everything that had occurred since. Only Venus and Mars hadn't bothered letting Cupid in on the whole truth.

And in the course of the past few weeks Quentin really had fallen for Sabrina: no magic or magic arrows involved.

"I can't believe *they* deceived me," Quentin whined. "My own parents!"

"I can't believe *you* refuse to believe I'm not Psyche!" Sabrina persisted, beseeching her aunts, "Tell him!"

Salem, who'd been circling the couch deliberately, finally said, "I can't believe you're Cupid. Prove it!"

Hilda, too, was beyond curious. She turned to her niece. "Sabrina, how do you know he really is Cupid? Okay, we know his mother's not mortal—now I know what the *V* really stands for—but what other evidence do we have?"

Sabrina looked at Quentin and shrugged. "My aunts need proof—then I just know they're going to come up with a plan to help you. And me."

Quentin nodded his understanding. He stood up, shed his jacket, and then his shirt. He turned around and unfolded his wings. They glistened!

Salem arched his back and leaped . . . backward!

Hilda approached gingerly. "Can I . . . touch your wings? And, well, I know you're sort of off-duty now. But you know my ex-fiancé, Drell? Have I mentioned him? Is there anything you can do . . . ?" Suddenly Hilda stopped short and looked around the room. "Where are your arrows?"

"I left them in the car," Quentin responded. "But about Drell . . . well, my mother thinks you could do so much better. . . ." Then Quentin stopped himself. What was he saying? Who cared what his mother thought! She'd lied to him!

Abruptly Zelda broke in, "You've got a problem communicating with your parents, Quentin. I think you and Sabrina can hash that one out on your own. Come, Hilda, let's get back to dinner."

"Wait!" Sabrina cried. "Aren't you going to tell him I'm not Psyche—that I'm a witch?"

As the women headed for the kitchen, Hilda

tossed back at Quentin, "She's a witch, Cupid. Really. She's not the Pysche chick you're looking for. I have her birth certificate and her whole family history. When you guys are finished, I'll show you the family tree."

Zelda added, "It's true, Quentin. Besides, if memory of mythology serves, Psyche had waist-length hair and didn't shop at J. Crew. And I don't remember any myth where Psyche pointed her finger to make things appear. Show him, Sabrina."

Sabrina smiled. "Thirsty?" she asked Quentin. Without waiting for an answer, Sabrina pointed up two thick shakes. "I made mine chocolate—yours strawberry."

Quentin's jaw hung open. Sabrina continued, "And I'm up for a snack. Don't you love those pigs-in-a-blanket things? Actually, they're Harvey's favorites." Instantly a tray of mini-hot dogs appeared—with mustard on the side.

"And in case you feel bow-and-arrow separation, I'll just spirit your archery case in from the car, okay?"

Quentin's hands flew up in the air—just in time to catch the archery case that Sabrina had, in fact, motioned in from his car, opened the door, and let in.

He gulped. "Stop. Stop. Okay . . . okay . . . I guess I believe that you're . . . that witch thing. But Psyche . . . I mean, Sabrina, me believing you doesn't change anything. My parents will come to get you. And they've got some pretty persuasive magic of their own. You might not be able to stop them."

Sabrina shuddered. The idea of being witch-napped to another dimension was not exactly how she'd envisioned spending the next several centuries. "You may be right, Quentin. I don't know if my magic would be any match for them. But yours would."

He shook his head. "I don't think so, Sabrina. How could I go up against the Goddess of Love and the God of War? Separately they're pretty powerful. Working together, they're indomitable. Besides, that's not really my nature. I'm a lover, not a—"

Sabrina interrupted to gently remind him, "But you're also their son, Quentin. And that counts for a lot. If you're really serious, I bet you can get them to listen to you. And this time you've got the truth on your side. No matter what their weirdo plans are, they've got the wrong girl. I'm not Psyche."

"The truth!" Quentin practically spat. "That means nothing to them! You have no idea what it's like to live with them, Sabrina. In this century you'd call them dysfunctional. She's always dreaming up some romantic scenario, he's always declaring war, and both of them want me to be more like they are. You don't know how lucky you are to live with your aunts."

Sabrina furrowed her brow. "Excuse me, you don't exactly have the lock on weird families. No one has the perfect family. In this or any other universe, realm, or dimension."

"You do," Quentin insisted. "Your aunts are great."

Sabrina sighed. "See, Quentin, that just shows how little you really know about me. My aunts *are* great, but did you ever wonder where my parents are? I'll tell you: My dad's in a book and my mom's in Peru—if I set eyes on her in the next two years, she'll turn into a ball of wax. Anything about that sound normal to you? Still, if I really needed them, I know that somehow they'd be there for me. In spirit, anyway. Just like I know your parents would listen to you."

Quentin was surprised at Sabrina's revelations, but didn't relate. He did have an idea, though. And a burst of enthusiasm. "There's only one thing that will save us. I'll run away! They can't take you back without me. The legend is Cupid and Psyche, not Cupid minus Psyche. If I don't go, you won't have to."

"How could you possibly not go back, Quentin?"

Obstinately he folded his arms across his chest and thrust out his chin. "I just won't, that's all." Warming to the idea, he added, "Besides, I want to stay here! It's cool here on Earth!"

Sabrina considered. "You're right. It can be pretty neat, but it's not your world, Quentin. I mean, talk about destiny. You have a job to do. Like my aunt Zelda just reminded you. You're supposed to deliver the gift of love to hearts too pure to be lonely. People in all realms need you. You can't just walk away from it. I mean, imagine a world without Cupid to believe in! It would be beyond sad."

Quentin scowled. "That's all very sweet, Sabrina, but what about me, huh? No one ever thinks of how *I* feel. I'm sick of being Mr. Goody Two-wings. Here in Westbridge, no one knows I'm Cupid, but I'm a star! I *like* being popular! Before you bribed me to play that last match fair and square, I was worshipped! Besides, I watch TV. I see that other Greek gods are doin' pretty well here. I mean Hercules has a movie *and* a syndicated TV show. Xena's got a series and a video. So why couldn't I? I'm cuter than they are."

Sabrina couldn't help giggling. Quentin really was cute. But completely misguided. "I think you're missing the point, Quentin."

But he was on a roll. "What about you, Sab? Ever think of a TV show? I mean, a sitcom about a teenage witch who casts spells on all her friends—how cute would that be?"

"I imagine it would be a big hit, Quentin, but I like to keep a low profile. Being normal kinda means a lot to me. . . ."

He interrupted, "That reeks! I love being the center of attention! Shameless self-promotion, that's my middle name. You really don't know a lot about me, do you, Sab?"

She shrugged. "Just the good stuff, I guess. The rest of what you've been telling me hasn't gotten a lot of publicity. It would sort of sully the myth. People want to believe in the Cupid on Valentine's Day cards. Speaking of which . . . stay right there, I'll be right back."

Abruptly Sabrina raced up the stairs to her room. When she came back a minute later, she handed Quentin a Valentine's Day card. It pictured a cherubic Cupid, poised to send his magic arrow on its romantic journey. "See this? I bought it for Harvey."

Quentin blushed furiously. "I *hate* those pictures! They were taken when I was a chubby baby. How would you like your baby pictures bandied about, all over the world?"

"This is so cute—you're embarrassed!"

Quentin chafed. "And as if that weren't bad enough, don't even start with those songs. 'Cupid's Revenge,' 'Stupid Cupid'—I've heard them all.

Sabrina was amused. "I guess your public image could use some updating."

Quentin shot her a quizzical look. "Speaking of images that need updating—what about yours? I mean, you're a witch. Where's your black pointy hat? I always thought witches prowled the Earth in the dark hours before dawn."

Sabrina educated him. "As opposed to you, who enjoys a completely positive image, witches have had a lot of bad press. But pointy hats? That went out years ago! I relate to what you're saying about the songs—if I hear 'Witch Doctor' or worse, 'Witchy Woman' one more time, I'll barf."

It was Quentin's turn to be amused. "I guess neither of us exactly lives up—or down!—to people's perceptions. But . . . uh . . . if you really are a witch, then we should have something else in common."

"What's that . . . ?"

Quentin sprung up and unbuttoned his shirt. "I'll have to dispense with this—and I guess you'll have to go to the broom closet and get what you need."

Instantly Sabrina understood. "I will need help, Quentin, but broomsticks went out with the pointy hats." Sabrina disappeared into the front hall closet.

A minute later the teenage witch reemerged pushing her trusty Hoover Upright vacuum cleaner.

"We're going for a ride," she called out to her aunts. "We won't be late!" Then Sabrina and Quentin stepped out onto the front porch. She positioned her feet on the base of the vacuum cleaner and gripped the handle. He exhaled and spread his glorious wings. She pointed the machine skyward; he took a flying leap. And they took off: up, up and away!

Chapter 11

☆

☆

"This is so fun!" Sabrina cried as she whirled high above the streets of Westbridge, piloting her vacuum cleaner.

"Groovy!" Quentin agreed, beaming. He'd extended his golden wings to their full ten-foot span. "I've never flown with anyone before, Sabrina—this is mega!" Then, way up in the moonlit sky, he reached over to hold her hand. Sabrina took one hand off the controls to clasp his. She was elated at the sheer pleasure of being able to share this part of her life with someone.

"Let's go above the clouds, where we'll be protected from the inquiring eyes of anyone on the street," Quentin suggested. "Can you do that?"

Truthfully, Sabrina had never flown quite that high. In fact, she was still a novice pilot. The first time she got behind the stick of the upright, she exceeded the speed limit and got a ticket from the witch police. Clearly there were speeding rules, but she wasn't sure about height limits. She glanced over at Quentin, who had a mischievous twinkle in his eye. The boy was persuasive.

"Oh, why not?" she answered. "Let's give it a go!" Sabrina followed Quentin straight up through a puffy, cottony cloud. Emerging on the topside of the cloud was beyond cool. She and Quentin seemed close enough to touch the stars, so crystal clear was the air. Not a witch police in sight. And, as Quentin figured, a winged Cupid and vacuum-cleaner-flying teenage witch were less likely to be spotted by random mortals who might happen to glance up into the evening sky. Sabrina felt amazingly free and comfortable with Quentin.

As if he could read her thoughts, Quentin ventured, "It must be a drag, having to hide the truth from all your friends, never being able to show off."

"It can be frustrating," Sabrina agreed, "but what I *can* share with them more than makes up for what they'll never know. And besides, I have my aunts and Salem to confide in—as well as my parents, in a weird sort of way."

"Where I live, everyone knows all about me. I have lots of friends, though I'm always flying off somewhere, bringing together deserving couples."

"You must have amazing tales to tell about the love stories you've had . . . an arrow in," Sabrina ventured.

Quentin swelled with pride. "All the great ones. Bogie and Bacall, John and Yoko, Tom and Nicole, Demi and Bruce, Dennis Rodman and himself. Well, that one was a mistake—the arrow boomeranged, hitting him twice."

Relating his past experiences to Sabrina, Quentin was forced to admit that he really *did* get a major kick out of helping people fall in love. Staying earthbound, always under wraps, *would* be giving up a lot. Unless, he thought, he had a dual identity, sort of like Clark Kent and Superman: popular student by day, Cupid by night. The concept needed work, but it could happen. . . .

"Quentin—look!"

"What?" He'd been so caught up in his daydreams, he hadn't realized Sabrina was trying to show him something. He followed her downward gaze. Through the cloud cover he could see they were hovering just above . . . his house!

And as bad luck would have it, his parents were outside. His mom was reclining in a hammock in the backyard, popping bonbons, reading some romance novel by flashlight. His dad was warring with the hedge clippers.

"Hmmm," Sabrina was musing. "I didn't know we had a street named Mount Olympus Lane in our neighborhood. I'll take a wild guess that we didn't—before you guys got here. And I'll take another, that we won't—after you leave."

Those were rhetorical guesses. But as long as they had inadvertently wandered over Pid "palace",

Sabrina knew what they had to do. She aimed her vacuum cleaner downward.

Severely unthrilled, Quentin hastily dipped down and followed her. With a thump, they landed in tandem in the backyard, right between Quentin's parents.

His dad reacted first. Only he didn't seem to get that Sabrina had flown there of her own accord. "Well, well, what have we got here?" he sneered. "I see you've revealed your little secret, Cupid. And even better, you actually managed to fly her here in something resembling a timely fashion. And, look! She brought a power tool from this century. . . ." He focused on Sabrina, less than kindly. "You won't be needing it, dear. Not that you won't be cleaning floors. Just that you'll be doing it on your hands and knees, heh, heh, heh."

"Martin! Enough!" Quentin's mom hopped off the hammock. Veronica affected a gushy friendliness as she strolled up to Sabrina and put her arm around the teenager's shoulders. "Don't mind him, Sabrina, dear. It's so lovely to see you. And aren't you thoughtful, bringing such a *practical* gift? Won't you stay for dinner? For the next several centuries?"

Quentin put his hand up. "Don't bother. I know all about your plans to make her a slave. We both know. So you can cut the phony sweetness. We came to tell you that we're not going. Neither of us. Right, Sabrina?"

But before Sabrina could answer, Martin, eyes flashing with fury, growled menacingly, "What is this insubordination? Who do you think you're talking to?" He took an ominous step toward Quentin, but Veronica stepped between them.

Veronica purred, "Quentin, darling, whatever are you talking about? Clearly, you've told Sabrina who *you* really are. And obviously, she's admitted who *she* really is. Or you both wouldn't have flown here on your golden wings of love. So, what's all this about you not going?" Veronica winked at Sabrina. "Of course you're coming with us. Your lives together will be—"

"Nonexistent!" Sabrina marshaled her strength and edged into the conversation. At Veronica and Martin's startled looks, she quickly added, "No offense, but aside from the horrid plans you have in store for poor Pysche, I'm not her. It's all been a case of mistaken identity." She eyed Quentin. "Tell them—or will I have to show them?"

Veronica dismissed her. "What could you possibly show us? We've already established that you're Psyche. Although . . . not quite as, don't take this the wrong way, but . . . not quite as ethereally beautiful as the grapevine had you."

Sabrina let the insult slide. She met Veronica's gaze with a determined stare. "You need proof that I'm not Psyche? Let's try this on for size." Deliberately, she placed her feet on the base of the vacuum cleaner, clasped the handle, and went for a swirl above the Pids' backyard. Just for fun, Sabrina turned the turbo power attachment on and skimmed the tops of the hedges off.

Martin's jaw dropped—the hedge trimmers he'd been carrying clattered to the ground.

"Is that enough proof for you?" Sabrina asked when she landed smoothly.

Veronica sniffed, "All you've proved is that power tools of the twentieth century are more advanced than we thought, like cooking techniques."

Sabrina shrugged and stepped off her flying accessory. She pointed to herself and levitated three feet off the ground. Then she spirited over to the hammock where Veronica had been relaxing. She picked up the box of chocolates and announced what was inside each: "Caramel in here, solid chocolate here, and pink gooey stuff that looks like liquid antacid in this one."

Suspiciously Veronica nibbled each one. Sabrina was, of course, right. Then the teenage witch made a few more points, just in case the Pids still didn't get it. She turned the hammock into a duck. She turned the hedge clippers into a goose. They quacked loudly and chased each other in circles. Sabrina was about to see what else she could transform when Quentin gently closed his hand over hers. "I think they get it, Sabrina."

Veronica and Martin—Venus and Mars—were gaping at her, speechless. Finally Veronica managed to stammer, "What . . . what . . . *is* she?"

"I'm a witch," Sabrina burbled brightly.

"A witch? But where's your . . . ?" All at once it dawned on Veronica that the vacuum cleaner was an update of the broomstick witches used to fly on. Her luminous eyes bugged. "And I suppose all that pointing at dinner the other night . . . that wasn't some new cooking technique. Your aunts must be, too."

Sabrina nodded. She told them about Hilda's discovery of their second-grade yearbook. "That's how we knew *you* weren't mortal. We just didn't know *what* you guys were—we thought maybe undercover witches. Or something."

Veronica bristled. "That's preposterous! I'm a legendary beauty. Witches are ug—" She stopped herself just in time.

Sabrina was smart enough not to react to the partial diss. She knew that many people still believed in the old *Wizard of Oz* caricatures. With time and education, she was sure perceptions would change. Turning to Quentin, she prompted, "But proving to you that I'm not Psyche isn't the entire reason we're here, is it? Don't you have something to say to your parents?"

Quentin quivered. "Nothing. It's not important."

Sabrina coaxed, "It *is* important. Communication is hyper-important. For all families, in any realm or dimension. Tell them how you feel. That's more persuasive than my magic, and you know it."

Veronica's maternal side surfaced. "She's right, darling, your feelings are very important to us."

Martin's grouchy side did, too. "Enough! If you have a beef—act like a man, put your dukes up!"

Quentin cowered and tucked his head under his wing.

Sabrina gently but firmly pushed the feathered attachment back and peered at Quentin meaningfully.

With Sabrina by his side, Quentin summoned up his courage and looked his parents in the eyes. In a quavering voice he finally told them how he felt. "I'm hurt. You betrayed me. You both lied to me. When you told me the legend of Cupid and Psyche, you made it sound like some fantasy romance— like I could finally do for myself what I've been doing for other couples over the centuries. Mom, you never told me you were jealous of Psyche! And that after I got her, you meant to turn her into an ugly, wretched slave! You and Dad used me." Emboldened, Quentin thrust his chin out, announcing, "And I refuse to let that happen. Not to Sabrina and not to me."

His dad thundered, "How dare you challenge authority? I am your father—you never talk back to me! I am the God of War!"

Once again Veronica interceded. Understanding filled her eyes. There was remorse in her tone, but also quiet strength. She touched her husband's arm gently and shook her golden-tressed head. "No, Martin, he's right. We did use him. I . . . I never felt right about that. We owe him an apology."

Quentin looked from his mom to his dad. For

once, his dad stopped raging. Instead, at his wife's touch, Martin suddenly softened. He regarded Veronica with something resembling love in his eyes.

Sabrina spoke up. To Veronica, she said, "Okay, here's what I don't get. Why would you be jealous of anyone? I mean, look at you! You're the epitome of ageless, timeless beauty." To Quentin and Martin, she said, "Right, guys?"

Quentin and his dad didn't have to say anything. Their eyes said it all.

Sabrina continued, "Look, I don't have to tell *you* that love is what makes people beautiful. You've got a really great son . . . and a . . . well, important husband. They both love you unconditionally. And if that weren't enough, you're Venus, Goddess of Love. Psyche, whoever and wherever she is, can't take that away from you. No one can. The myth is with you!"

Martin inched closer to his wife and circled her in his overdeveloped arms. Veronica's eyes had been downcast, but now she smiled warmly—sincerely this time—at Sabrina. "In a silly kind of way I'm sorry you didn't turn out to be Psyche after all, Sabrina. Anyone would be proud to have you as a daughter-in-law someday—even if you don't cook or mop floors."

Sabrina grinned. "Hey, I'm only sixteen. It'll be a long time before I'm *anyone's* daughter-in-law. But I know this. Whoever does end up marrying Cupid won't steal anything from you—not your beauty or your son."

At that, Veronica drew Quentin close to her. To the mortal eye, for that moment at least, the Pids approximated an actual loving nuclear family— even the duck and the goose Sabrina conjured up nestled calmly at Veronica's feet.

Suddenly Sabrina felt a strong urge to get home. She mounted her vacuum cleaner and got ready to point it homeward. "Well, I better be going. I guess I'll see you in school tomorrow, Quentin."

Sandwiched between his parents, smiling hopefully, he waved at her.

Only Quentin wasn't in school the next day, or the one after that. The effects of his invisible love arrows, however, lingered like an annoying cough, as Sabrina noted glumly. Not to mention how it was negatively affecting the quality of education.

Principal Conroy and Vice Principal Lautz were so deliriously happy, they added "No homework Mondays, Wednesdays, Thursdays, and Fridays" to join the still-in-place Tuesday proclamation. Mr. Pool and Ms. Ehrenhart were team teaching. There were only so many ways, Sabrina was discovering, to legitimately pair cooking and biology. Coach Robbins had coaxed Ms. Hecht to ditch ancient history and focus on famous figures in sports history.

The students, of course, couldn't have been more elated. The lunchroom looked like a multiplex on Friday nights: couples everywhere. Sabrina had taken to eating by herself in the quad.

The school gym had been turned into Valentine's Day dance central. Heart-shaped decorations were affixed to the ceiling, bleacher seats, and basketball hoops, in preparation for Saturday's shindig. Everyone was going. Everyone except Sabrina, that is.

All through the past few weeks, even before she knew about Cupid, Sabrina had stubbornly refused to give up on getting back her life. Every few days she'd invite Jenny to the mall or over to her house—each time, however, Jenny turned her down, citing a prior commitment. Whose name was Harvey.

Sabrina continued to leave messages on his answering machine and stuff funny little greeting cards into his locker outside of homeroom. Although Harvey never acknowledged receiving them, he apparently didn't mention them to Jenny. Sabrina took that as a potential good sign.

She remained hopeful, until, that is, she overheard Harvey and Jenny's plans to spend spring break together. Spring break was months away! That's when the teenage witch started to despair.

So what if Sabrina now knew *why* everything had happened? She had no clue how to undo the damage. If it even could be undone. She needed Quentin for that.

But by Thursday of that week, there was still no sign of him and Sabrina could wait no longer. She *had* to see him—he owed her, big time! She'd

143

helped him confront his parents—now he had to help her get her life back! That afternoon Sabrina raced home after school, intent on flying to Quentin's house. She only knew how to find it by air, so she'd need her vacuum cleaner.

In her anxiety to get to the front hall closet, she waved off Hilda and Zelda, who were calling to her from the living room. "Not now!" Sabrina yelled out. "I've got to do something—I'll see you later."

But just as she lugged the upright out of the closet, Salem jumped on it and motioned toward the living room. "I think you'll want to come inside first, Sabrina."

She whirled around: Quentin was sitting on the couch, between her aunts. He smiled sheepishly over his shoulder at her. "I . . . I came to pick up this. . . ." He held up the white shirt he'd left at her house, the day they went flying together. "And to say . . ." Embarrassed, Quentin glanced at Hilda and Zelda. They took the hint, scooped up a protesting Salem, and left the room.

Sabrina raced over. "Am I glad to see you, Quentin! I was just about to fly to your house. Where've you been? I really need to talk to you—"

"I need to talk to you, too," he interrupted. "Look, Sab, I came to apologize for getting you all mixed up in my crazy family crisis. You didn't deserve it. But I also came to thank you. Without you, I never would have found the courage to face them. And just like you said, they actually listened to me—even my dad! He actually admitted that by standing up to him I proved worthy. Of something. Anyway, they might even go for family counseling when we get back home. Isn't that cool? We really learned a lot from our trip here."

"That's great, Quentin. But I still need to talk to you about—"

"And lastly," he interrupted, leaning forward, "I came to say goodbye, my love. We're leaving tomorrow."

Sabrina panicked. She clutched Quentin's shoulders. "Wait—you can't go! You have to undo the damage! You have to uncouple the couples. . . ."

Quentin backed away, surprised. "Damage? I made people happy."

"That's not the point! Look, Quentin, there's a reason witches don't cast love spells, especially not on mortals."

Quentin started to get up from the couch. "Maybe you're just jealous, Sab. Making people fall in love is the one thing you *can't* do—and I can."

Sabrina grabbed his elbow. "But just because you *can* do something doesn't mean you *should*. And besides, here in Westbridge, your aim was not true. Cupid is supposed to bring together couples who are meant for each other, but just don't know it. You didn't do that. You just shot your arrows haphazardly. Okay, I know you wanted to separate me and Harvey. But aside from that one, whoever else got hit fell in love with the person next to her. That can't be right."

Suddenly Quentin shot Sabrina a sheepish look.

"There's, uh, kinda one thing I haven't told you, Sab. As an archer, I still do okay, but with my invisible love arrows? Well, the truth is, I've been sort of rusty lately. Especially when I'm shooting from a distance. It's really affected my success quotient over the past century or so. That's the reason for the high divorce rate. So, chill—in twenty years or so, if the couples I brought together weren't meant to be, they'll divorce."

"Twenty years!" Sabrina's voice cracked with stress. "I can't wait that long for Harvey! Quentin, you've got to do something now, before you leave. Saturday's Valentine's Day! There's one more day of school this week—you have to come back and break up these couples. You just have to."

"Sabrina, I can't undo the love spells. There's no way."

☆

Chapter 12

☆

Way! Way! There has to be a way!" Sabrina was frantic. Facing twenty years without Harvey *and* without her best friend was unthinkable! As in, it wasn't going to happen. Not if she could help it. "Quentin, you say you really . . . like me a lot. If that's true, you've got to try. For me."

"I don't just *like* you a lot, Sabrina, I love you."

"Then help me."

Unbeknownst to Quentin and Sabrina, Salem had slithered back into the room. Just then he made his presence known by jumping on the arm-rest of the couch and starting to clean himself.

"Salem—do you mind?" Sabrina was annoyed. "We're in the middle of a major crisis here. Can you do that someplace else?"

"I could, but then I wouldn't be a whole lot of help to you, would I?"

Sabrina gripped the underside of Salem's chin, forcing him to look at her. "What are you talking about, cat?"

Salem wrested his head from Sabrina's grasp. "All I'm saying is . . . reading is *fun*-damental!"

"I get such a kick out of your talking cat, Sab!" Quentin exclaimed.

"If only he knew what he was talking about, I'd get a kick out of it, too."

Salem bristled. "I take exception to that, Sabrina. I'm trying to help you. Read all about it!"

"Read all about what?" Exasperated, Sabrina called out to her aunts. Hilda and Zelda quickly came in from the kitchen and listened as Sabrina detailed her dilemma. "There *is* something we can do about it before Quentin leaves, isn't there? Salem knows, but he's refusing to make sense."

Zelda's hands were on her hips. "Maybe Salem wants you to figure it out for yourself."

Sabrina shot her aunts her best beseeching look. "Please, guys, just this once, *help* me figure it out."

Her soft-hearted aunt Hilda relented first. "What's Salem saying?"

"He's quoting some public service commercial. Something about reading being fundamental."

Quentin broke in, "Well, that seems clear enough to me, Sabrina—don't you have some kind of book about witchcraft? Didn't you say your father lived in it? Or some weirdo thing like that."

Sabrina's jaw fell open. "My spell book? The

answer's in my spell book? But how could that be? There *are* no love spells."

Zelda sighed. "Right. But that doesn't necessarily mean the corollary always holds true."

Sabrina paced the room. "Aunt Zelda, I'm more confused than ever—not to mention *out of time.* For once, can you just tell me what to do, using normal language?"

"Oh, all right," Hilda answered for her sister. "What she means is, if you look in the right places, there may be something about undoing unjust love spells. But that's all I'm saying. You'll have to figure out the rest on your own."

"What rest?" Salem snorted. "You just told her all there is to—"

Sabrina didn't hang around. She grabbed Quentin's arm and raced up the stairs.

"Cool space, Sab!" Quentin enthused, looking around her room. For once, Sabrina didn't even mind him invoking that exclusive-to-Harvey nickname. Or even feel weird about having him there. She had no time for either.

She lugged the book out from under her bed. "Here, we'll look through it together. Quentin?"

But he was entranced, staring at himself in her full-length mirror. "I *am* cuter than Hercules, don't you—"

"Sit!" Sabrina commanded him. "You're going to reflect on someone other than yourself for once—a lot of others, in fact."

Reluctantly Quentin turned away from the mirror and sat down beside Sabrina. "Introduce me to your dad," he insisted as she turned the pages.

Sabrina waved him off. "Later. First, we're looking up love. And how to get us out of the mess you made."

They were so busy poring over each page, they didn't hear Salem slink into the room—until he announced, "Cut to the chase, kiddies. It's under *U.*"

Sabrina looked up quizzically. *"U?* Why would it be under *U?* Why not *L,* for *Love?"*

Salem shook his head. How naïve these witchlets could be. *"Un*do. *Un*just. *U.* Don't they teach you to alphabetize in the twentieth century?"

Without bothering to thank the cat, Sabrina flipped the pages quickly. She finally came to the *U* section. *"To undo unjust love spells . . ."* She skipped over the long explanations of what those were. *". . . you must find a way for the truth to pierce the hearts of the nondestined lovers."*

The truth? How could the truth pierce their hearts? Quentin ran his hands through his curly ringlets. "Maybe it's referring to that truth potion you threw at me," he suggested.

"Sprinkles. Not potion," she corrected him. "But that has to be eaten, ingested. You can't pierce people's hearts with them."

Suddenly Quentin's eyes twinkled. He grasped Sabrina's elbow. "But my arrows can. What if . . . no, forget it. Dumb idea."

"What? Speak! Quentin, even a dumb idea is

better than no idea. Which pretty much describes what I've come up with so far."

Quentin took a deep breath. If what he was about to propose worked, he'd lose Sabrina forever. He couldn't even come back for her. But . . . the way she was looking at him right then? Her eyes were filled with hope—for getting back together with that Harvey chump. Oh, well, no matter how he felt, he couldn't turn her down.

"All right, here goes. What if we coated my arrowheads in something sticky, then dipped them in the truth sprinkles—then, I'll just 'reshoot' all the couples? That way, the truth sprinkles would get under their skin at least. It isn't exactly the same as ingesting them, but . . ."

Sabrina bolted up from the floor. "Quentin, that's brilliant! Dumb, but brilliant! I mean, your love arrows are invisible . . . this is nuts."

Quentin grimaced. "Maybe so. It also may be your only chance. Sab."

Sabrina and Quentin went to school together the next day. She had a complimentary case of the jitters. He was equipped with his truth-sprinkle-coated love arrows and his cocksure attitude.

As they entered the school building, Sabrina led Quentin to the principal's office. Practicing on the adult couples made sense. If it didn't work, what did anyone have to lose? Using their own individual magic, Sabrina and Quentin entered the office silently: No one heard them.

151

They came upon Principal Conroy perched on the corner of Vice Principal Lautz's desk. He was handing her a bouquet of flowers and smiling at her lovingly. As the principal leaned in to give his beloved a peck on the cheek, Sabrina silently chanted, *"Those who aren't meant to be, with this arrow, we separate thee!"* Then she tapped Quentin on the shoulder: *Shoot, now!*

Expertly he grabbed a truth-sprinkled—albeit invisible—arrow, swiftly aimed at his quarry, and released. Sabrina held her breath. She only allowed herself to exhale when jarringly the vice principal jerked her head away from Principal Conroy, demanding, "What are you doing? I'm allergic to flowers! Are you trying to give me an allergy attack?"

Irked, he retorted, "What made you think these were for you? I wouldn't give you flowers if you were the last woman on earth!"

"I wouldn't take them if I were . . . you're a lame excuse for an administrator, anyway. What are those ridiculous 'no homework days'? What do you think we're running here? A party? This is a school!"

Grinning victoriously, Sabrina and Quentin dashed out of the office before anyone could see them—and headed directly for their science classroom. There, no surprise, they found Ms. Ehrenhart writing a "scientific" recipe—for angel food cake—on Mr. Pool's blackboard.

As Mr. Pool sidled up to the home ec. teacher,

and put his arm around her, Sabrina whispered, *"Cooking and science both are cool, but if you don't love him, you'll release Mr. Pool."* With that, Quentin took aim at the pair.

Instantly Ms. Ehrenhart yanked Mr. Pool's arm off her shoulders and shot him a disgusted look. He returned it with one of his own, picked up the eraser, and swiftly wiped her recipe off his blackboard. Without a word, she marched out of the room. Mr. Pool shook his head. Then he shrugged and began to write today's lesson on the blackboard. It was about photosynthesis.

Sabrina couldn't conceal her delight. This was working!

Quentin swelled with pride—this was his idea, and his handiwork. He was brilliant! "Next victim?" He looked to Sabrina, who knew exactly where they were going: the athletic field to uncouple Coach Robbins and Ms. Hecht.

Within minutes they had another success!

Then they aimed for their first student uncoupling. They found football captain Larry Carson counting Rebecca's freckles. She was giggling coyly. Sabrina recited, *"A football he does fling, an arrow she will sling—if it wasn't meant to be, bells will no longer ring."*

And with a flash of an invisible arrow, they stopped. Rebecca backed away from Larry, sniffing, "You'd better go. I just realized we're not right for each other. I'm sorry, but we can't see each other anymore."

Larry grinned. "Nothin' to be sorry about, babe! I am outta here!" Sabrina had never seen Larry run so fast, not even for a touchdown.

Sabrina couldn't help herself—she threw her arms around Quentin. "This is so cool!"

He beamed. "I'm a cool guy, Sab. Don't know why you couldn't see that before."

"All right, all right, let's go—we've got work to do."

And all through the day they did. Sabrina and Quentin snuck up on unsuspecting couples and, two-by-two, uncoupled them. In their classrooms, in the gym, in the lunchroom. The words, "I'm . . . with you? What was I thinking?" reverberated throughout the corridors and classrooms.

Sabrina almost hesitated when it came to Libby and Melvin. Wouldn't it be sweet revenge to keep them together? But she decided not to jinx her success. Fourth period Libby and Melvin had math together. They'd actually changed their seats to be closer. Now they sat side by side in the last row. Perfect!

Sabrina and Quentin snuck in the back door of the classroom and crouched low so as not to draw attention to themselves. Under her breath, Sabrina chanted, *"To live as Libby Bibby would serve you right, but even I cannot perpetuate such a blight."*

With that, Quentin aimed and fired—it took but a nanosecond for Libby to shoot Melvin one of her patented withering glares. "Ugh! Who gave *you* permission to exist? And invade my personal space? You're the world's biggest dork!"

Melvin adjusted his glasses and fired back at her, "And you're the world's biggest snob!" Then he waved his arm frantically, yelling to their teacher, "I have to change my seat—now!"

"Yesss!" Sabrina shouted as she jumped up and high-fived Quentin. "Okay, one to go! Let's find 'em!"

When she'd think about it later, Sabrina couldn't be sure if Harvey and Jenny were last on the list consciously or not. For their own reasons, both she and Quentin almost dreaded doing it.

If it worked, it meant Harvey and Jenny were never right for each other—and Sabrina would have her life back to the way it was before Quentin had arrived. Which was what Quentin dreaded.

If it didn't work, it meant that Harvey and Jenny really *did* belong together after all. Sabrina's nightmare.

Fifth period was study hall for Sabrina, Harvey, and Jenny. Usually they spent it together, out in the quad. That's where Jenny and Harvey were now cuddling, sharing a bag of trail mix, and going over their history assignment. Sabrina and Quentin ducked behind the bushes.

Sabrina closed her eyes, and whispered intently, "*If truth is destiny and destiny is truth, this arrow will tell; my best girlfriend, and the boy of my dreams . . . whatever happens, I wish you well."* She refused to open her eyes, lest a tear fall.

Because Harvey and Jenny were sitting so close together, piercing their hearts should have been a snap, but inexplicably, Quentin's shot completely missed! Not very convincingly, he whispered, "Ooops!"

Sabrina's eyes flew open. The sight she saw unnerved her: Harvey put his arm around Jenny. Sabrina glared at Quentin. "Ooops? What do you mean, ooops? Your arrows may be invisible, and my eyes were closed, but even I could see you didn't even try to aim that one."

Quentin admitted sheepishly, "I know. But if my aim isn't true, it's because my heart's not in it. I really love you, even if you're not Psyche, even if the legend doesn't say so. Even if you're a witch. Even if I'm leaving—I still don't want you to go back to him."

Sabrina sighed and dropped to the ground. Quentin squatted next to her. "Quentin, you think you love me, but you barely even know me."

"I know you're beautiful. And bewitching. And I also know—admit it, Sab—you think I'm pretty adorable, too. What else do we need?"

"Tingling. We need tingling. We don't have it."

"What?" Quentin was truly confused.

"Look, Quentin, you're right, you are . . . really, *really* cute. But love is more than just being attracted to someone. Love is so many things. It's deep friendship. It's being able to tell that person anything, and know he'll always be there for you. And it's tingling. . . ."

"I know your deepest secret," Quentin interrupted. "Harvey doesn't."

"You know I'm a witch. But being a witch isn't what defines me. It's only part of who I am. You haven't been around long enough to really be my friend. And love without friendship can't exist. As Cupid, I'd think you'd know that."

He made one last plea. "So I'll stay here. I'll learn more about you. We'll be friends—and then we can fall in love."

Sabrina leaned in toward him. His huge blue eyes seemed so innocent just then. She allowed herself to run her fingers through his silky ringlets.

"You can't stay here, Cupid. Nor should you want to. Don't you know how lucky you are? Most people spend years trying to figure out what they're supposed to do with their lives. But you already know. And it's a great job! I heard the joy in your voice when you were telling me about all the great love stories you nurtured. And think of the perks! You can inhabit *any* body. You're ageless. You get to travel that whole time-space continuum thing, bringing the gift of love wherever you go . . . all in all, Cupe, not a bad gig if you can get it."

His eyes were downcast. "But what does it matter if I can't bring you . . . ?"

"I belong here, on Earth. With my aunts, with Salem, with my friends . . ."

Quentin was crestfallen, but he knew the rest of the sentence. "With Harvey, right?"

"I don't know for sure that we'll always be together. But for now? It kinda feels right. We're definitely friends, and we've got the tingling thing going. And right now, I'm really missing him. So could you try your arrow again? Please?"

Quentin knew when he was defeated, but he wasn't leaving without exacting something in return. "Okay, I'll do it, but you have to do something for me, Sab."

"No bribes, Quentin. Not this time. Shoot fair and square. And accurately!"

"Okay. Just promise that you'll at least E-mail me. My address is Cupid@greekgod.myth. And in a hundred years or so, if it's over with Harvey, and the Psyche thing doesn't work out . . . well, never forget me, Sab. Because no matter what you think, you really do have a friend in me."

Impulsively Sabrina leaned over and gave him a peck on the cheek. This time her fingers weren't crossed behind her back.

"What was that for?" Quentin asked, surprised.

"Hey, you're a legend. I want to tell my grandchildren I kissed Cupid. No, really, you *are* a friend. Friends work together to right wrongs—like you and I just did. And one more thing, Quentin? If you and your family ever do find Psyche—go easy on the girl!"

"You got it, Sabrina." With that, he heaved a

heavy sigh and let his arrow go. One last final arrow.

Bull's-eye!

Instantly Harvey and Jenny pulled away from each other. Dazed and confused, they looked around awkwardly, not knowing what to say. Jenny spoke first. She gathered her books. "I . . . I'm not sure what's going on here, Harvey. But I feel twelve ways from uncomfortable. Where's Sabrina?"

"Hey, I'm clueless, too. Talk about feeling weird! Where *is* Sabrina?"

"Right here, guys. I've been right here all along." Sabrina stepped away from the bushes and walked up to them.

Jenny and Harvey lit up and bounced off the bench. They both ran to embrace her as if they hadn't seen their best friend in ages. Come to think of it, they really hadn't.

Jenny was bursting with excitement. "Sabrina! I . . . I don't know what's been happening, I just know I miss you! We have so much to catch up on. . . ." Jenny burbled on, while Sabrina beamed. "It feels like a really long time since we've gone to the Slicery together, I can't wait!"

"Me, either, Jenny, me, either!"

Just then the bell rang. "Gotta go," Jenny called, bolting toward the school building. "I *cannot* be late for English. See you guys later."

Harvey made no move toward the school. He ran

his fingers through his wavy hair: his earrings glistened.

"Don't you have a class to get to Harvey? I mean, don't we both?"

"Uh, yeah, but wait a minute. Anyway, you're allowed two tardys before you get in trouble. Look, Sab, I don't know what came over me these past few weeks."

"I do."

"You do?"

"I mean, well, just forget it, okay?"

Awkwardly Harvey turned to rifle through his backpack. He pulled out a stack of cute greeting cards, one written on tissue . . . and a bunch of phone messages which he'd obviously copied off his machine. Sabrina recognized them right away.

"I got these. . . ." he stammered. "I saved them."

She smiled. "I'm really, really glad you did, Harvey."

Sabrina took Harvey's outstretched hand and headed off to class. But suddenly something told her to turn around. Quentin was still in the bushes.

Sabrina slipped her hand out of Harvey's. "Hang on, I'll be right back."

She scurried over to Quentin. "I have to know something before you leave, Quentin. Did you just shoot another arrow—I mean, at me and Harvey?"

Quentin looked at her longingly. "I didn't have to, Sabrina. You and the Harvey dude . . . well, I can't predict the future, but you don't seem to need any help from me. I'm going to where I can do some good."

"You already have, Quentin. More than you'll know."

He took off his leather jacket and his shirt. "Keep these for me, Sab, okay? Just in case I come back sooner than anticipated." And then he leaped up off the ground and flew away. The last Sabrina saw of him was a pair of golden wings, heading straight up into the clouds. She waved.

In a flash Harvey was beside her. "Who are you waving at, Sabrina? A bird, a plane . . . ?"

Sabrina gazed into Harvey's gentle hazel eyes and smiled. "Cupid. I'm waving at Cupid." And then she kissed him—and tingled.

Harvey grinned at her. "You're amazing, Sabrina Spellman. Anyone ever tell you that?"

"Lots of people . . . but I like it best when you do!"

He coughed, then cleared his throat. "So, uh, the dance tomorrow night? We're still going, right? Together, that is?"

Sabrina's heart sang. "You're asking me to the Valentine's Day dance?"

And then he uttered the words she'd been waiting all this time to hear. "Who else would I go with, Sab?"

About the Author

Randi Reisfeld is the author of *Clueless: True Blue Hawaii, Clueless: Too Hottie to Handle, Clueless: Cher Goes Enviro-Mental, Clueless: Cher's Furiously Fit Workout,* and *Clueless: An American Betty in Paris.* She has also authored *Prince William: The Boy Who Will Be King, Who's Your Fave Rave? 40 Years of 16 Magazine* (Berkley, 1997), and *The Kerrigan Courage: Nancy's Story* (Ballantine, 1994), as well as several other works of young adult nonfiction and celebrity biographies. The *Clueless* series, duh, is totally the most chronic!

Ms. Reisfeld lives in the New York area with her family. And, grievously, the family dog.

jewel

With color photos!

Pieces of a Dream

Everyone loves Jewel! But not everyone knows the amazing fairy-tale story of this intelligent and gorgeous 24-year-old singer's rise to fame.

Find out the real story about Jewel's childhood in Alaska, where she lived on a homestead without running water and electricity. What's her love life really like? And how did a singing gig at a coffeehouse lead to a CD that has sold more than eight million copies?

Read this brand-new book by
Kristen Kemp
to find out!

From Archway Paperbacks
Published by Pocket Books

2010

@café

Meet the staff of @café:
Natalie, Dylan, Blue, Sam, Tanya, and Jason.
They serve coffee, surf the net,
and share their deepest darkest secrets . . .

Novels by Elizabeth Craft

Available from Archway Paperbacks
Published by Pocket Books

POCKET
BOOKS

1430-02

Sabrina
The Teenage Witch™

Salem's Tails

What's it like to be a powerful warlock, sentenced to one hundred years in a cat's body for trying to take over the world?

Ask Salem.

Read all about Salem's magical adventures in this new series based on the hit ABC-TV show!

#1 CAT TV
#2 Teacher's Pet
#3 You're History
#4 The King of Cats
and
Salem Goes to Rome

Look for a new title every other month

A MINSTREL BOOK

Published by Pocket Books   1495-01